The As~~cension Trilogy~~

Book 5

Conquest & Conflict

Gary Richardson

First originally published by Gary Richardson 2023

ISBN 979-8-3507-1565-1 (Paperback)
ISBN 979-8-3507-1566-8 (Digital)

Printed in the United States of America

To my beautiful wife Crystal. How you've managed to put up with me all these years while still supporting my dreams is amazing. I love you with all my heart.

Gary Richardson

Series Reminders

What follows is a summary reminder of all places, names, and other key identifiers which is
coupled with a pronunciation guide in the previous books. Any places, names, or similar identifiers included in this book will have a similar pronunciation guide, so no fretting. Any new characters, places, or items introduced in this book will not appear in this list but will have an appropriate pronunciation guide in the book near its first appearance to avoid any potential spoilers.

Pronunciation guide:

Rishdel (Rish-del)

Corsallis (Cor-sol-is)

Kirin (Kear-in)

Bjiki (Bee-zee-key)

Mechii (Meh-chi)

Kaufmor (Cough-more)

Norsdin (Nor-sh-den)

Nefarion (Ne-fair-e-on)

Skeel (Scale)

Triandal (Trin-dull)

Izu (Is-ew)

Arissa (Ah-riz-sa)

Leza (Le-z-ah)

Baolba (Bowel-ba)

Derkar (Der-car)

Ami (Ah-me)

Ailaire (El-air)

Ellias (El-i-us)

Raiken (Rye-ken)

Sagrim (Sag-rim)

Trylon (Try-lawn)

Rhorm (Roar-mm)

Macadre (Ma-cod-dre)

Riorik (Re-or-ick)

Cyrel (Sear-el)

Shadrack (Shad-rack)

Nordahs (Nor-duh-sh)

Nectana (Neck-ta-on-ah)

Heilstur (Hill-st-ur)

Aqutarios (Ah-k-tar-e-os)

Grue (Grew)

Kelig (Kale-ig)

Gromard (Grow-mard)

Tyleco (Tie-le-co)

Do'ricka (Door-ick-ah)

Argrip (Are-grip)

Perigrine (Pair-eh-grin)

Rakish (Rack-ish)

Tanion (Tan-ya-un)

Ori (Or-ee)

U'gik (Ew-gick)

Veyron (Vay-ron)

Yorid (Your-id)

Bostic (Boss-tick)

Jayn (Jane)

Droth (Draw-th)

Brem (Brim)

Dylo (Die-low)

Theon (They-on)

Daldon (Dowl-don)

Kerros (Care-o-ss)

Draynard (Dre-nard)

Morthia (More-thigh-ah)

Fielboro (Fail-bore-o)

Asbin (As-bin)

Deaijo (Day-hoe)

Wuffred (Woo-fred)

Brennan (Bren-in)

Dava (Day-va)

Klienheart (K-line-heart)

Via (Vie-ah)

Freca (Freh-ka)

Zox (like "socks" but with a z) Coway (Cow-way)

Arin (Are-in) Aurochs (Or-awk-s)

Neddit (Ned-it) Barbos (Bar-bo-s)

Valstrand (Veil-strand) Alaricea (Ah-lar-eye-see-ah)

Pan (Pan) Magnus (Mag-n-us)

Ammudien (Ah-mew-dee-in) Algon (Al-gone)

Whilem (Will-um)

Chapter 1

As dawn broke over the walls of Kern, the unsuspecting citizens of the town began to emerge from their doors. As they started the day like any other, merchants headed off to the town square to peddle their goods at their stores and stalls. Womenfolk hurried along behind them, hoping to get the best picks from each vendor. The guards changed shifts as those who had taken the night watch were relieved by the next assigned for that duty. Initially, the day started without a hint of the threat that loomed just beyond the city's walls.

The King of the North had positioned his troops around the city of Kern under the cover of darkness. Each group of his soldiers was placed to ensure no citizen or messenger could flee the city all while inflicting maximum fear on the city's soon-to-be besieged residents. His plan was not one of destruction but occupation. The safety of Macadre was far from Kern, and for his plan of invasion to succeed, he knew that he would need a base to operate from close to the front. Kern was close, and it was thought to be the easiest to take between it and Tyleco.

The unseen king had been careful to keep his troops just beyond the horizon's edge as the light began to creep across the land of Corsallis. He wanted his presence to be a complete surprise to the unsuspecting townspeople, so he had to remain hidden from the night watch. The plan was for the gnolls to the south of the city to attack and scare farmers and travelers as they tried to leave the city. Their screams would be the signal for him and his larger collection of forces to advance from the north, revealing them to people of Kern.

It did not take long for his plan to take effect.

Eager to get out and tend to their fields that lay just outside the city wall, a family of farmers made their way to the southern gate. The guards atop the gate had no idea that the gnolls were lying in wait outside and were very accustomed to seeing the family so early, day after day. So, as it was their routine, the guards mindlessly opened the gates without a second thought as they sent the family outside to their undoing.

The middle-aged man and his three sons casually passed through the gate with their cart and tools in tow. It was a journey they had taken countless times over the years. Rarely had there ever been a problem or a threat, so the familial patriarch and his offspring paid little attention as they moved over the rough, cart-worn path of a road that laid under their feet.

The family owned a small plot of land that they had cultivated crops on for generations, so much so that it was all very routine and scheduled. During the warmer seasons, the crops were planted in the more distant fields. Then, during the colder seasons, the crops were planted in the fields closest to the city. This meant that the family could work in the mornings before it got too hot during the warmer periods and were able to reach the fields and home faster during the colder seasons. Unfortunately for this farmer and his children, it was currently a warmer season, so their destination was going to take them a bit too far from the city wall today.

The father led the way, and his three teenage children followed behind, taking turns pulling the cart as they argued over who would have to pull the cart back after it was full of produce. The bickering was a distraction for the family leader. It had finally worn on his nerves to the point that he turned to chastise and discipline his children, but in doing so, he turned his back to the attacking gnoll headed his way.

Just as he pointed his finger toward his children and began to get their attention, the children looked on in horror as the gnoll struck. The hairy beast came racing on all four legs toward the unaware man. And in a flash, the gnoll sprung onto his hind legs before slashing at the unsuspecting human's back. The wounds were deep, and blood rushed from the new openings in copious amounts. The man only felt a searing pain as he fell to the ground under the shock of the sneak attack.

The attacking gnoll wasted no time as he spun around and leaped onto the back of his downed target. The force of the gnoll's weight striking the wounded man's back caused the human to yell out in pain as he spat up the blood that was now beginning to fill his mouth. The gnoll looked directly at the man's children before using its powerful jaws to crush his victim's windpipe, causing the man to die. Sure that the man was dead, the gnoll turned its attention back to the children and glared at them as it licked the blood from around its snout.

One of the children froze in terror while another, the youngest of the three, broke down in tears. The third son, and also the oldest, bravely grabbed a long-handled spade from the wooden cart as he prepared to defend himself and his brothers. But that plan quickly fell apart as the howls and growls from other gnolls seemed to surround them. The other gnolls slowly walked forward from their hiding spots and revealed themselves to the boys. The realization of just how badly they were outnumbered and the gruesome end that awaited them was enough to change all of their minds.

The oldest brother dropped the crudely made tool as he retreated to his brothers. Then, as a group, the trio turned and fled back toward the city gates, screaming all the way. They never looked back to see the gnolls retreat as they ran past the guards who rushed to see the source of such commotion. The guards just stood at the gate and looked down the path as far as their limited human eyes would let them but saw nothing but the faint silhouette of a cart off in the distance.

***

"Boys! Boys!" one of the guards shouted as he tried to get a response from the frightened children. "What happened? Where's your father?"

His questions fell on deaf ears as the three brothers were still too terrified and mortified by what they had just seen. The sudden and unexpected death of their father and the overwhelming number of gnolls were still concepts their younger minds struggled to comprehend.

For the next several minutes, the guards were so consumed by trying to console the wailing children while still trying to get answers that they left the southern gates opened and freely allowed people to pass out into the wilderness. The guards were completely unaware of the dangers that lurked just beyond the gates. The children's comatose state left the guards and the citizens of Kern totally ignorant of the threat hiding outside.

However, it did not take long for that threat to become known.

A dozen or so people had left through the gate after the boys had returned, but they all came running back screaming after finding the father's corpse on the road or having witnessed another gnoll attack. For many of the people, it was the first time they had seen a gnoll, and their descriptions to the guards left something to be desired.

13

"It was like a giant hairy dog that walked upright," one witness told the guards.

"It was half man, half wolf," another described.

"I think it was a werewolf," one woman declared.

The guards were unsure what was being seen or even how many of them were out there, but one thing was certain, the gate needed to be closed immediately. Several of the guards set about moving the heavy wooden gate doors, while the others hoisted the massive wooden beam that would be placed across them to brace and secure them. Meanwhile, another guard sitting atop the wall near the gate sounded a horn to signal for trouble. The horn would alert the other guards to be on watch while it let the residents know to stay in the city.

The horn sparked a flurry of activity inside the now sealed city. Guards armed themselves and moved into defensive positions around the top of the wall and near the gates. Merchants closed their recently opened stores and joined the other citizens running through the streets to seek cover in the larger, sturdier buildings.

***

The sounding of the horn was exactly the signal the northern king had been waiting for. Upon hearing the trumpeting sound, the armored king signaled his commanders to move his forces from the north closer to the city, bringing his army's might into full view of the now alert guards.

The self-appointed king's troops marched in unison. The thundering sound of their footsteps could be heard even before their bodies could be seen. The guards on top of the walls protecting Kern turned to look in the direction of the booming noise. Many of their hearts filled with dread as the troops of an invading army filled the horizon. And it did not take long for that dread to spread throughout the city as word passed from person to person about the massive force positioned just north of the city.

Panicked people ran through the streets with more urgency than before when they thought there might be only a few villainous individuals outside of their city. The threat of an entire army was much more serious. A bevy of guards emerged from the guardhouse in full armor and took defensive positions outside the northern gate. As the last of the armored guards passed through the gate, the guards inside the city walls moved to quickly close it behind them.

The large wooden city gates slammed shut on both ends of the city, sealing the city's inhabitants inside. To further increase the city's security from the forces outside, the guards lowered a very heavy iron portcullis in front of the wooden gates, along with a massive timber beam that was slotted through locking channels behind the gate to keep them from bursting open from an assault.

Still, more guards poured out from the guardhouse and down the city streets as the top of the city wall was nearly overrun with a show of force. Kern's leader, Lord Shiron[1], a cousin of Tyleco's Lord Veyron, thought that if maybe he put his forces on display, that it would scare off any soldiers of a weak heart in the forces now camped just beyond his city's walls. However, the guards did not report seeing any deserters fleeing, but rather, the entire group in the north advanced closer to the city.

The emboldened king was smart though. He advanced his troops nearest to the city as he could without putting any of his forces in range of the city guards' bows or crossbows. For now, his troops remained untouchable by Kern's watching forces.

---

[1] Pronounced "Shear-on"

His troops were eager to attack the town, but he knew that this was not an opportunity to attack—this was an opportunity to spread fear. He commanded his troops to halt and stand their ground. He wanted the townspeople to realize that fleeing the city was not an option, something many had already figured out after the gnoll attacks earlier, but more importantly, he wanted them to know that help was not coming. So far, the city had not sent out birds to ask for help or warn of his troops' arrival, something he was certain they would have done immediately, but apparently not.

His archers remained hidden in their positions west of the city and vigilant in their watch for any courier birds released but saw nothing. There were no obvious holes in the solid stone walls that encircled the city for the birds to fly through as in Nectana, so it was believed that the birds would be released in the city and fly over the walls, giving the archers ample time to draw their strings and snipe their targets from the sky. And, in fact, they were right. Birds did get released from behind the walls before flying over them on their routes, only no birds had been released today.

Lord Shiron was a proud man, too proud to ask Lord Veyron for help as the two families had been squabbling over who was the rightful heir for generations. Plus, for all he knew, the forces outside

Kern were nothing more than marauders from Brennan looking to prey

on his people. After all, Brennan was a town run by bandits as a safe

haven for bandits. To ask for help from Brennan, to him, was like

inviting the marauders to raze his city and loot his storerooms. And

being a proud human leader, he felt it was beneath him to seek aid from

the elves, dwarves, gnomes, and halflings of Corsallis. They were

considered lesser folk to him. This only left the barbarians, which he

looked at as little better than bandits and considered them more

mercenaries than anything, or the other human town of Fielboro at the

southern edge of the Kaufmor region. He suspected the barbarians

would demand payment for their help, while Fielboro was too far away

to provide any timely assistance given the circumstances. So instead of

sending word to anyone, the proud city leader opted to try and weather

this storm on his own. At this point, the group had not made any

demands or attempts to attack the city, so he felt comfortable that Kern

could withstand a small siege before the group got hungry or bored and

left.

***

The elven king of Narsdin waited and waited for the birds to fly. He wanted the city, and more importantly, the city leaders, to know that they were surrounded and alone before he made his demands. Little did he know the depth of the pride that Lord Shiron felt about his race and his family's ongoing debate on inheritance. Hours passed and not a single bird flew. His troops were beginning to get restless. He knew the time to act was now, or else he risked the entire plan.

"Perhaps if I make my demands and put on a little bigger display, then I can force them to send birds out. Then they will know that I am their only option for survival," he thought to himself as he adjusted his plan in his head.

He motioned for his orcs to move from the back of the lines to the front and join him. A call could be heard echoing through the ranks to 'send up the orcs' as it spread from one group to another and moved to the back of the massive group still standing in the field. Several minutes later, the packs split apart to make way for the orcs who were lumbering forward. Eventually, about a dozen large orcs stood around their heavily armored leader.

The armored king stepped forward and began walking toward the city gates. The orcs loyally followed behind without question or fear. It did not take long for the small group to get into range for the archers on top of the city walls, but none dared to fire a shot since no aggression had been shown. The armored division of guards standing outside the gate readied their weapons and fell into a defensive formation.

Cyrel came to a stop several feet from the guards at the gate. He looked over them briefly before lifting his head up and studying the guards on the wall, who now had all of their many arrows and bolts pointed in his direction. Satisfied with what he saw, he slowly and casually lifted both of his hands to shoulder height to show anyone watching that he was not holding a weapon. He kept his hands held up as he spoke.

"I am the king of Macadre in the Narsdin region. Make no mistake, this is an invasion, but I mean you no harm. My goal is to once again unite Corsallis under one rule. What good is a king with no subjects? I would rather embrace you into my realm and my army than kill you, but let there be no ambiguity, I will kill you if I must. Please send word to your city leader or leaders that I seek their immediate surrender, but any resistance or aggression will be matched threefold against you. My army is far superior to yours both in numbers and power. Your best chance of survival is capitulation, not violence. My troops and I will wait until morning for an answer. After that, we will take the city by force."

He paused a moment to let his words sink in before continuing.

"When your leadership is ready to accept my terms of surrender, send a lone messenger to my camp dressed in white, unarmored and unarmed."

He did not wait for a response or even a confirmation. Once he had said what he wanted, the invading king turned on his heels and casually walked back toward his camp. The orcs followed without hesitation as the city's archers carefully kept their aim on the beasts but were sure to keep a strong hold on their strings to prevent an unintentional arrow from getting away and sparking a war.

A short walk later, Cyrel returned to his troops.

"Set up camp," he commanded, sparking a flurry of activity from his troops.

The troops focused on his tent first. It was the largest tent in the camp, with enough space for a private sleeping area and a separate place for him to meet with his generals to discuss strategy and status.

As soon as his tent was complete, the King of Narsdin summoned his generals to meet him inside as the troops continued to set up the rest of the camp.

Once everyone had gathered inside his rather posh tent, complete with ornate furniture and lavish decorations, he addressed his army's commanders.

"Kern has until morning to surrender peacefully before we force them into submission," Cyrel said as he started the discussion.

"Are you certain that is the best move?" one of the generals asked. "That gives them several hours to prepare for a drawn-out siege."

Being questioned by his subordinates was known to rile the short-tempered king, but the general spoke before thinking better of the decision. However, today was his lucky day as the obviously annoyed king only took a deep breath before giving a heavy sigh at the general's question.

"Yes, this is the move I have deemed appropriate, and it would do you well to remember that my orders are above reproach," the general's king sternly replied before addressing the crowd once again.

"It is my desire to take Kern with minimal force and therefore minimal losses. There are many cities for us to take so it's imperative to conserve our troops as much as possible."

"And what of your promise of peace to the people of Kern?" asked another, who was obviously confused by his king's offer to the besieged town's leaders.

"Hmph, peace is but an illusion, " the armored king huffed. "However, it is an illusion we need to maintain for now. To have a drawn out fight with Kern risks our troops that we'll need moving forward. Other towns and races are sure to fight back eventually. And conscription from a recently occupied city is not likely to yield great support when needed the most. Deception is paramount to our success, and then, when we have control of Corsallis, we can truly teach them the price for their treachery. They will see how their hatred toward us has fanned the flames of an even stronger hatred toward them. Those who resist will know no mercy, and the rest will serve us in the most demeaning of tasks."

His commanders were beginning to see the genius in his plan and the ruthlessness that they had all come to expect from their leader.

Chapter 2

Unaware of the events unfolding to the east, Ammudien and Rory

approached the gates of Tyleco. Ammudien, being a gnome and not a

human, was hesitant to walk so openly into the town of his great heist,

but Rory looked at the sturdy walls of his home with a welcoming gaze.

It had been days since he had left in pursuit of Wuffred and his friends,

so he was eager to return to his home, family, and position.

The guard captain was worried that his unexpected and

unexplained absence would have caused his wife much duress and could potentially cause difficulty for him upon his return but, at the same time, his personal fears were insignificant compared to the impending threat of invasion. His call of duty compelled him to put his personal fears aside and return to Tyleco for the safety of those he was sworn to protect.

"Are you sure I shouldn't make myself invisible?" Ammudien nervously asked as the pair drew nearer the gates.

"No," Rory replied, "I think it is best if you stay just the way you are. If you use your magic to be unseen only to be discovered or revealed later, then you would likely be seen as a liar and untrustworthy."

"Untrustworthy?" Ammudien blurted out in shock and surprise. "Are you ignorant to the ways of your people? I am a gnome; most humans would consider me untrustworthy for the simple fact that I am not like them. Even you must admit that you have had your own prejudices toward those different than you."

The gnome's words shamed the city guard. It had been socially acceptable for so long to look down on the other races that the guard captain had adopted a similar racist attitude that was shattered when he was accepted and befriended by Ammudien and the others. So many stereotypes and ignorant beliefs about the other races were wiped out as Rory's eyes had been opened to the truth—they were all alike and no one race was above or better than any other.

"I see your meaning," Rory replied. "But still, I think it is in our best interest to be open and honest with Lord Veyron about your presence and the rising tide of violence that comes this way."

"And what of the shield? Would you have me return that?"

"No, my dear friend, that shield is yours. It belongs to your people, not mine. If you want to make something invisible, that would be it."

The two slowed their pace as they discussed what was involved in using Ammudien's magic to hide Sagrim's Shield and how the tiny mage could hide it from sight but not from touch. Even if the shield was hidden and he was not, there was still significant risk that it would be found if the guards searched the gnome at any point.

"What about a spell that makes you look human?" Rory asked Ammudien.

"Most magic doesn't really work that way. Besides, illusion and transformation spells like that were banned long ago for obvious reasons. Too many people were doing what you want to do and making themselves look like someone else to commit crimes and frame others. And, especially in the time of the Ascendant Lords, Sagrim took no chances that someone could be in disguise around him or disguised as him to steal his beloved shield."

"What about making the shield invisible and hiding it out here? We could come back to retrieve it later."

"I'm not taking the chance of someone else finding such a powerful item by leaving it laying around in a field."

"Right. Forget I even suggested that."

"I wish I could."

Finally, Rory conceded and asked what Ammudien would suggest they do.

"I still say invisibility is our safest route," started the gnome, "but I agree with your assessment that if we want to gain the most credibility with your Lord Veyron, then my presence should not be a secret. The challenge with that, though, is that it is unlikely I would be given an audience with your lord unless I were searched for weapons— which would result in the discovery of the shield that I desperately do not want to see returned to the storeroom and locked away again. So, as I see it, we only have one option."

The gnome paused for dramatic effect with success as he looked at Rory.

"And what option is that?" Rory excitedly asked his friend.

"Well, I say we put the shield in my pack, I make the pack invisible, which makes the shield inside invisible too, and then we strap the pack to the front of your waist. If you get searched, they will most likely take the obvious weapon on your hip, check your boots for daggers, and maybe the sleeves of your tunic. But, it is unlikely that they will pat down your groin. This may let us gain entrance to the city, seek an audience with your city's lord, and return to our friends, all while keeping our possession of the shield a secret."

Rory thought about Ammudien's plan for a moment but could not come up with anything he felt was better. Eventually, Rory agreed with the gnome's plan but kept his doubts about the plan's success to himself.

The two newfound friends ducked off the road leading to the city's gate before drawing any more attention from the guards they were rapidly approaching. After finding suitable cover behind a series of leafy bushes, Ammudien set about putting his plan into action. He already had placed the shield in his pack, so now it was only a matter of drawing the necessary runes around the pack now sitting on the ground and completing the spell.

Rory watched on in amazement as he saw the pack one moment and witnessed it vanish as Ammudien moved the runes along the height of the leathery pack. He had seen only a glimpse of Ammudien's magical power in his short time with the group, so each exhibition left him in a state of awe with his mouth agape.

A few short minutes later, an invisible pack containing an invisible shield was securely fastened to Rory's waist, and just like that, the pair were once more following the road to the gates of Tyleco.

***

Riorik, Kirin, and Nordahs were sure to use their elvish nimbleness and agility to move more quickly to Rishdel than Ammudien and Rory had been able to toward Tyleco. The elven village was a great distance further from the oasis compared to Tyleco, not to mention buried deep inside a thick forest. Time was of the essence, so they had to move fast but not without caution.

"Do you think it's safe for us to return?" Riorik asked his childhood friend.

"Probably not, but do you think we have a choice?" Nordahs asked rhetorically.

"Yeah, I know," Riorik sighed because he knew that as a Ranger who abandoned his guild, his life was forfeit upon his return to the village. He could only hope that he and Nordahs would be able to convince the elders to hear them out before being put to death.

"I suppose we should get our stories straight at least," Nordahs suggested as the two moved swiftly across the land.

"What do you mean?" Riorik questioned, unsure of his friend's thoughts.

"Well, we were tasked with killing Wuffred and now he's dead. Maybe we can save our necks if we tell them that we completed our orders," Nordahs theorized aloud to his friend.

"So, you want to lie and pretend we did the very thing that sickened us? And then, you want to besmirch Wuffred's sacrifice by hiding his efforts in thwarting the very person that threatens us all?"

"Yes." Nordahs' answer was short, to the point, and absolute. There was no hesitation in its delivery and no doubt in its tone.

Riorik stopped dead in his tracks and looked at his friend with dismay and a slight sense of disgust.

Nordahs, who had expected this type of response from his fiercely loyal friend, was quick to stop and attempt to explain the psychology behind his approach in hopes of convincing his friend of its merits.

"If we tell the truth, we will be deemed traitors to the guild and put to death while Wuffred's sacrifice will be ignored and called nothing more than 'what he deserved' by the elders. You know that to be true as much as I do. But, if we tell them that he fled and we pursued him before achieving our mission's goal, then perhaps that will win us enough trust, or even glory, to get an audience with the elders where we can tell them about your father and his approaching army. That is the best chance we have of gaining support from the guild and defending our home."

"Can we, maybe, leave out the part about the army marching this way being led by my father?" Riorik questioned. "Besides, how would we explain how we found out his identity? If we say that Kirin

31

was working with the enemy, then we may have saved our lives but we'll have cost my brother his."

This immediately got the attention of Kirin, who had also stopped to hear the discussion among the two friends.

"Wait, what?" Kirin asked curiously at the mention of his death.

"Think about it," Riorik answered. "If we tell the guild elders that you helped our father and that he is planning some large-scale invasion or war, then you will be branded a traitor and co-conspirator to his murderous intent. The elders will execute you as a spy if nothing else. In fact, your presence and association with us jeopardize our lives too if we tell the elders of your involvement and efforts."

"I see your point," Nordahs answered, having quickly realized Riorik's words were true. "Then we should keep your father's name out of it for the time being, for all of our sakes."

"But what about the greaves?" Kirin asked, curious about the pair's plan for the once missing armor now covering Riorik's long, slender legs.

"I say we keep these a secret too," Riorik quickly quipped, not eager to see his prize taken away by the prideful guild elders who would surely want to wield the armor's power for themselves.

"I concur," Nordahs said, agreeing with Riorik since he too knew the elders would waste no time in claiming the greaves for themselves. "In fact, Riorik, you will probably want to take them off and put them in your pack before we reach the village gates. It's probably best that they not be seen at all while we are there."

"Or," Kirin interrupted, "I could wear them under my robes. They'd never see them under there."

The older brother was undoubtedly curious about the gifts of the armor. Having seen them in action, he wanted to experience it for himself but saw few other opportunities to wear his brother's prize.

The suggestion caught both Nordahs and Riorik by surprise. Kirin had shown no interest in the armor, aside from his intellectual interest that helped him to find the breastplate buried under the oasis. Riorik immediately felt conflicted. Kirin was after all his brother, but at the same time, until recently, Kirin had been helping what was now obviously the enemy. Riorik wanted to trust his brother but found it difficult to do so now that trust was required. Nordahs, on the other hand, was not apt to trust Kirin just yet. He knew Riorik's brother well, but Kirin's association with Cyrel still stung Nordahs so soon after their deadly encounter.

"No offense, Kirin," Nordahs started, "but I'm not sure we are truly ready to entrust such a key item with you just yet. Your loyalty to your family is beyond doubt, but Cyrel is still your family so I'd feel better if Riorik just hung on to them for now."

Nordahs' words were a great relief to Riorik. He wanted to say the same thing, but the thought of telling his older brother no was a daunting task to the young elf. But his relief was to be shortlived.

Nordahs turned to Riorik.

"Right, Rio?"

Riorik was now put on the spot. He felt as if he would betray someone dear to him no matter what he answered. If he agreed with Nordahs, he would be betraying his brother, but he if agreed with Kirin, he would be betraying the one friend that had remained beside him through everything bad in his life, including the recent death of their other friend.

In the end, Riorik could not bear the thought of parting with the armor. He could not bring himself to relinquish them to Kirin or Nordahs. It had nothing to do with trust or recent experiences, only that he wanted them for himself. Was this the dark side of the armor or just his own personality? Riorik did not know, but he was certain that he wanted the armor to stay with him. He thought fast for a response.

"Kirin, this has nothing to do with trust," he started, "but I think I'll hang on to them. I have used them in battle and know what to expect from them, so if we find ourselves in some trouble then, I feel, I am the best suited to use them in our defense. If Nordahs had asked me to give them to him, this would be my answer to him as well. You are my brother and I would trust you with almost anything else, but the severity of the situation and the great risk that we face returning compels me to ask you, and you too, Nordahs, to trust me with your lives right now, and that means me keeping these for the time being."

He hoped that his answer would satisfy both of his companions, and it seemed that they accepted his answer.

And indeed they had. Nordahs was glad to see Riorik not give in to Kirin's request, and Kirin knew that his odds of getting the armor were low, so Riorik's answer came as no surprise to the elven wizard.

"Well, I guess that's settled. We should get back on our way then. Yeah?" Kirin suggested.

The other two elves quickly agreed before returning to their graceful and effortless sprint across the countryside.

***

"Halt! You two, stop right there!" one guard yelled at Rory and Ammudien as they neared the gated entrance of Tyleco.

The pair stopped, unsure of the cause for the guard's alarm and aggression.

A group of lightly armored but heavily armed guards quickly filed out of the gate and encircled Ammudien and Rory.

"What's the meaning of this?" Rory questioned loudly as the guards readied their weapons. "Do you know who I am?"

"Of course, we know who you are," came the response from the guard.

Rory struggled to look through the barricade of soldiers that blocked his view of the gate, but he was unable to see who had answered him. This caused the already flustered guard captain to become more irate at his current treatment.

"Then you should know that I am the captain of this city's guard and this is a most undignified welcome for someone in my position. I demand that you stop this foolish display before I see you flogged," Rory yelled out in anger and embarrassment.

"You mean, you *were* the guard captain," the voice replied as the soldiers stepped aside and let their new leader pass through their ranks.

Finally able to see who he was really talking with, Rory attempted to diffuse the situation.

"What do you mean '*were*', Lieutenant Feigh[2]?" Rory asked of his second-in-command.

"That's Captain Feigh now," Rory's counterpart replied arrogantly. "After Lord Veyron's prize shield was discovered missing and you with it, it did not take our grand leader long to know that you had stolen it and fled like a coward. I was promptly promoted to your position and given strict orders to arrest you on sight for the theft of Lord Veyron's family heirloom."

Feigh's words initially caught Rory by surprise. At first, he thought about what audacity it took for Feigh to accuse him of stealing

---

[2] Pronounced "Fay"

such an important item, but that outrage was quickly replaced by fear once he remembered what was strapped around his waist.

Now, Feigh approached Rory and leaned in, talking to the former guard captain in hushed tones. Only hushed enough that the soldiers could not hear him but loud enough to ensure that Rory and his strange gnome companion could fully hear his words for maximum comprehension.

"Tell me what you've done with the shield, and I will let you both hang quickly. Otherwise, you will leave me with little choice but to have you tortured. And I'm sure your tiny friend here would love that. I bet the rack might even stretch him out to be almost as tall as you."

Rory had always despised Feigh, who no doubt had a hand in helping Lord Veyron reach a conclusion that included Rory stealing the shield for himself. And now, all that he had heard about Feigh from among the other guards and the complaints that Rory chose to overlook were all the more real and vivid as Feigh's words continued to ring in Rory's ears.

But, as angry as Rory was and as repellant as Feigh's new authority was, Rory knew that he had to take this chance to get an audience with his beloved lord.

"Feigh, listen to me," Rory started in a soft tone, almost pleading with his captor. "I need to speak with Lord Veyron. I did not steal his shield but know who did. There is more to this shield than you or I knew, and if I don't speak with our glorious leader, then we all risk the lives and safety of everyone in Tyleco."

Feigh just shook his head in response to Rory's request.

"Really? That's the best you can do? You sound like every other thief ever arrested. The only way you see Lord Veyron is as the last thing you see from the gallows. Lord Veyron does not trouble himself with the wild ramblings of thieves and traitors."

Quick to assess the situation and desperate to find a way out, Ammudien spoke out.

"What about me? Can I see Lord Veyron? I am not wanted for theft and only accompanied this man since running into him on the road. He said he was returning here, so I walked with him so that I would not be alone and could enjoy some conversation, something one does not often find when walking by one's self."

Captain Feigh stared at the oddly dressed gnome. Feigh was accustomed to seeing gnomes as gnomish vendors frequented the city to peddle their wares, but none were dressed like the mysterious gnome standing before him now.

Feigh pondered his thoughts for a brief moment before deciding to investigate further.

"And what business would you have with our city's lord?" he asked Ammudien with a somewhat skeptical tone.

Thinking fast, Ammudien opted to play toward his fellow gnomes' tradecraft.

"I am looking to open a new route of trade with my family's business, and I figured what better way to find out what trinkets and baubles would interest the nobility than asking those in charge. In fact, I can tell you exactly what kind of jewelry the nobility in Kern prefers."

Ammudien, by way of Rory, knew of the tension between the family lines that ruled Tyleco and Kern, so he hoped the guards would be aware too and seize this opportunity to get something over on their demonized cousins. If little else, he hoped it would add some legitimacy to his claim, despite it all being a lie.

His ruse was working. Feigh was interested in Ammudien's claim about Lord Shiron in Kern. The devious new guard captain was always looking for ways to improve his favor with Lord Veyron, and Ammudien's claim was the next way for him to achieve just that, or so he thought.

The newly appointed captain rubbed his chin as he briefly contemplated his next move.

Feigh looked at the gnome and winked.

"We may be able to come to some arrangement then," he said with a smile before he turned and walked away from the pair.

He approached one of the soldiers that had encircled them and issued his next set of orders.

"Take the ex-captain's sword, and take him to a holding cell in the guardhouse. He still has the information I need. And, as for the gnome, escort him to my office and stay with him there until I arrive. He may have other news from abroad that Lord Veyron may be interested in, but I need time to verify his claims first."

"Aye, Captain," was the soldier's response in confirming his new orders.

Feigh walked back toward the city gate while the soldiers moved to execute his wishes.

Chapter 3

Word of the northern army's demand quickly reached Lord Shiron. The invader gave an ultimatum of surrender or death and only hours to decide. The prideful human still refused to reach out for help but struggled to see a path to victory in the face of such overwhelming opposition with only the troops at his current disposal. Regardless, surrender was never an option. His family had controlled Kern for generations, but he knew that if he abdicated to the invader, then he was sure to lose any hope of finally being recognized as the rightful heir and being crowned king of the humans.

"Send in my advisers," Lord Shiron commanded to the guards standing nearest the doorway.

The guard nodded before pointing at someone outside in the waiting area and waving them into the grand room where Lord Shiron awaited.

The group of older men dressed in bright white robes entered the gilded room surrounded by large windows that flooded the open area with bright white light. Their feet shuffled them across the floor as the light reflected off their shiny bald heads. Lord Shiron's advisers made their way to his side before uttering a single word.

"What would you ask of us, Lord Shiron?" the lead adviser asked.

"You all know of the threat that sits just beyond our walls. Would you have me fight, flee, or capitulate?" their aged leader asked of the men that had influenced his every decision since coming to power as a teenager.

The advisers huddled together at their lord's question and chattered away for several minutes as they each contemplated their options and tried to come to a consensus. However, on this point, the elderly statesmen could not agree. Some wanted to surrender for the sake of sparing lives, mainly their own, while others wanted to fight for the honor of Kern.

"If we surrender, then this horde will just march on other cities. But, if we fight, even if we lose, then we might aid those who may later honor our sacrifice. There is glory in death, just as there is in life," one of the hairless mentors argued.

"As if one of these other heathen towns would honor us," another adviser countered. "For all we know, this horde is one of their doing, probably Veyron and his Tyleco thugs. They'd sooner see our bones bleached under the sun than honor our noblest of sacrifices. Our honor means nothing to them. If we are to live, we must fly the flag of surrender."

Eventually, their chatter led to squabbling, which turned to bickering before turning into an all-out brawl as the two factions began hurling insults at one another. It was indeed a stressful time, and it seemed the group of old men had let it get the best of them.

"Silence!" shouted Lord Shiron in an attempt to stop the geriatric fight unfolding before him.

But the elderly men's blood boiled with the rage of youth as they ignored their sworn leader and continued to fight. The fight was far from fierce, and the aged statesmen risked injuring themselves more than one another, but that did little to dissuade them in their anger. At one point, one adviser tripped over his own robes and fell to the floor before clutching his hip and crying out in pain. And, like Lord Shiron's command, the injured man's cries were ignored by the others as the altercation carried on.

After laughing at the old men's pathetic attempts at violence, Lord Shiron eventually waved toward his guards to break up the entertaining but futile scrap. Lord Shiron had hoped for guidance from the old men but instead had only gotten mildly entertained and no closer to an answer to his current dilemma.

"Throw these fools in the dungeon for a bit. Maybe that will remind them of their role in my court so the next time I ask for their input, I might actually receive it," Lord Shiron commanded his guards who promptly escorted the shouting men out of the grand room.

"Hmm," Lord Shiron thought to himself once the commotion had died down, "I am still no closer to a decision about these invaders.

I do not see how we can win, but I do not think that I can sit idly by and do nothing. If we surrender, my people could face a fate worse than death."

The conflicted leader struggled with his thoughts in silence before finally landing on what he felt was a solid solution.

"Summon my generals to the war room," he demanded before storming off out of the gilded hall and on toward his war room.

***

"Tell me where the shield is, Rory," Captain Feigh demanded of his previous mentor.

"I already told you, I followed a stranger out of town who had been acting bizarrely and whose story seemed farfetched. I was doing my job, not stealing Lord Veyron's things. I don't know where the shield is because I didn't take the damn thing."

Feigh looked down at his prisoner, unsure if Rory's story was true or not. Feigh had never known the once-illustrious Captain Cooper to be a liar or a thief, but he knew that if Rory was no longer a suspect in the theft, then his new-found rank among the guards would likely disappear too. This put Feigh in quite a predicament. He wanted to keep his new authority, but at the same time, he struggled morally with

47

the consequences Rory would face otherwise. Feigh was, by all accounts, an unscrupulous guard that would often take bribes to look the other way or hassle those who did not pay his fees, but he often tried to draw the line at corporal punishment, prefering it be reserved only for those who truly deserved it. And, in this case, he was not so sure that the former captain was so deserving.

"You have to know something. I do not believe it was a coincidence that you disappeared at the same time as the shield. Give me something so that I may spare you more shame and humiliation," Feigh continued, hoping that Rory might either confess, true or not, or that he may at least rat out a co-conspirator in hopes of getting himself a lighter punishment.

"Look," Rory started, "as I've said before, there was a strange human that showed up talking about bandit attacks, gnolls, and elves. His story didn't add up to me, so I followed him out of town. He met up with some other strangely dressed people out near an oasis a few days' journey from here. There was what looked like an argument from my vantage point, and the strange human I had been following was killed. I assume he's the one who stole the shield and was killed for it, rather than paid for it by this other person at the oasis. But, before I could get a closer look, a storm blew in and forced me away to seek shelter. By the time the storm passed, and I was able to return to the oasis, the others had disappeared. I returned to Tyleco emptyhanded and only learned of the shield's theft when you told me. I simply thought the human's story was fishy—little did I know what else he might have been involved in."

Rory was familiar with techniques used by liars, both good and bad ones, that he had interrogated over the years as a member of the guard, so he applied those techniques that were more successful and hoped that Feigh would not detect his attempt at deceit. He made sure to maintain direct visual contact with Feigh as he spoke, tried to add enough detail to his story but was careful not to say too much, and he made sure to try and tell a concise story without stuttering, stammering, or pausing as if he was trying to think of what to say next. Rory wanted to make sure that it seemed he knew what to say because it was what he experienced and not just what he wanted Feigh to hear.

Feigh, also familiar with the way to know if someone was lying or not, found himself still struggling with Rory and his testimony. Captain Feigh could not detect any signs of dishonesty in Rory's body language or speech, but there was just something about the former captain's story that he could not rationalize.

"So, you followed this stranger for several days without any proof that he had done anything wrong, and at no point did you see this stranger with the shield or any other goods that might connect him to the shield's theft?"

Rory knew that Feigh was still suspicious, but there was little else Rory could say without implicating himself or Ammudien in the shield's disappearance. Rory thought about his answer for a moment before responding but was careful to appear as if he were thinking about his pursuit and not scrambling to find an answer that would not lead him to the guillotine.

"I can't say that I did," Rory eventually answered. "I was careful to keep my distance during the pursuit so that I could observe the target while remaining unnoticed, but that meant being far enough away that I was unable to see things in great detail. I only continued my pursuit because it became apparent that his story about traveling with his family was false. If he lied to me about that, I wanted to know what else he may have lied about and what his true intentions were in coming into the city not once, but twice. And, when he had the meeting with the other individual at the oasis, I was still too far away to hear what was said or if anything small may have changed hands. I think I would have noticed a shield, even at that distance, but I do not recall seeing anything like that."

"This individual visited the city twice?" questioned Feigh as he began to believe Rory's story a little more.

"Yes," Rory replied. "He came one day and purchased various goods from the market, claiming that they were needed to help a family member who had been wounded in an ambush by some gnolls outside the city. This was shortly after we had killed a gnoll just outside the gate, so it seemed plausible and the items purchased seemed to support his story. But he returned to the city the next day just to speak with me. On both occasions, he was escorted through the guardhouse and directly past the armory where the shield was stored. And, now that I think about it, as he was being escorted out on the first visit, he actually asked specifically about the shield. I didn't think anything about it as many people ask about it the first time they see it. But now, knowing that the shield was stolen the next day, it does seem odd. Especially since he returned the next day for no real reason other than to

51

supposedly express his 'thanks' for the previous day's treatment. Ask around, the other guards will tell you the same thing."

This was the icing on the cake in Rory's mind. Rory knew that Ammudien and Wuffred had stolen the shield during the second visit, but thanks to Ammudien's invisibility spell, nobody knew the gnome had even entered the city. But Rory knew that Wuffred had interacted with multiple guards on both visits who would confirm Rory's story. From there, Feigh should be able to reach the conclusion that Rory was trying to lead him toward.

"Hmm," Feigh thought as he contemplated Rory's answer. It certainly seemed plausible to the new captain that Rory was telling the truth, but the one thing that Rory's story was missing was any evidence that exonerated Rory. Feigh decided to press Rory on that point.

"I will talk with the other guards to verify your story, however, what proof is there to say that you are still not somehow involved?" Feigh commented. "What proof can you give to show that you did not put the stranger up to returning the next day and that the two of you did not conspire to have him smuggle the shield out of the city before you both ran off with your ill-gotten prize?"

Feigh's prisoner had not thought of this latest angle of guilt that was being thrust upon his character now. It had caught Rory by surprise, but it should not have. It was an approach he had used numerous times interrogating suspected thieves and brigands during his time as the guard captain. How it had slipped his mind was intriguing to him, but he knew that he had a bigger priority right now—trying to convince Feigh of his innocence.

"Sadly, without the stranger here to speak for himself, there is little else I can say or do to prove or disprove my involvement in this fiasco. I must put that part of my fate in your hands and hope that my service to this town and our lord, combined with my character—something you should be very familiar with—is enough to garner me at least some faith and trust."

Rory was constantly aware of his involvement, and the fact that the shield in question currently hung from his waist, dangling in the air between his legs as he sat on the rock-hewn bench with his hands carefully placed over the invisible package.

"I guess we will see what the others have to say and go from there," Feigh replied before turning to the other guard who had remained in the room to witness the interrogation.

"Go and find the guards who were on duty at the gate on the day of the shield's disappearance. Do not tell them anything or ask them anything. Only inform them that I have summoned them to the guardhouse," he ordered the other guard, who quickly nodded in acceptance before heading out to complete his new mission.

Feigh followed behind the guard as they exited the room. Feigh could be heard telling the guards outside the room to keep watch over his prisoner while he went off to question the gnome who was in his office.

***

Ammudien sat in the simple wooden chair opposite Captain Feigh, who sat in his more expertly crafted chair positioned behind the wooden table that served as his desk. The diminutive gnome could barely see over the top of the table, much less the stacks of scrolls, the quill and ink jar, and the oil lantern that covered much of the table's surface. The small mage craned his neck to see over the clutter in a feeble attempt to make eye contact with the human that controlled his immediate destiny.

"Tell me again, how was it that you came to be in the company of the other human?" Feigh started.

Ammudien immediately recognized Feigh's tone of skepticism and distrust in the question. But the green-skinned foreigner did not believe that his friend Rory would have buckled so easily or so soon to give up the shield or the gnome's involvement in its disappearance. Ammudien decided to play Feigh's game. After all, to the highly intelligent gnome, humans were easy to read and deceive.

Ammudien retold the story they had given Feigh when questioned at the gate about how the two had just met by coincidence on the road between Kern and Tyleco and that the gnome knew nothing of the human's past or suspected theft.

Feigh listened to the story, trying to catch the gnome on any discrepancies, but the sharp-witted gnome was careful to be consistent. Feigh felt that deep down the gnome was lying, but he had no proof and Ammudien's consistency gave him no new leads. It was time for a different approach, the guard captain determined.

"So, you say that you are a merchant, yes?" Feigh asked.

"That's right," Ammudien answered "My family has a business back in Mechii that we are looking to expand, so I am going around to other towns, looking for opportunities to peddle our wares to a broader audience."

"And you said that business would be scroll and parchment production, right?" Feigh asked, hoping to catch Ammudien in a lie since the guard captain knew good and well that the gnome had mentioned jewelry previously.

Ammudien almost laughed at the human's poor attempt to deceive him. It took everything the gnome had not to smile or smirk with satisfaction at his triumph over Feigh and his pitiful attempts.

"No, no, no," the gnome began with a deliberate tone of disgust and offense at the suggestion of such a pedestrian profession one might expect from a high-end merchant. "My family only deals with the finest of gems and jewelry. For generations, my family was the sole provider of enchanted goods to the magic guilds of Mechii, but in recent years, our competition has grown so our local demand has faded, leaving us with no choice but to look beyond our city's walls to keep the ages-old business going for future generations."

Feigh's attempt at deceit to catch Ammudien's deceit had failed, but the guard captain was persistent. He decided to try one more tactic in an attempt to throw the suspicious gnome off.

"And do you have any samples of your wares that I may inspect?" Feigh asked his guest.

"Sadly, no," Ammudien answered quickly and bluntly.

"With the risk of bandits and brigands on the roads, my family did not think it worth the risk of sending me out alone with a cache of valuables for display purposes only. Instead, I am here with the purpose of determining what finely crafted goods might be of interest to your city's higher ranks and what simple enchantments they might be willing to pay for. With that information in hand, I am to return home to Mechii where my family will create a collection of goods to meet those desires and then we are to return with our goods to sell. Since we have dedicated our art to the local guild for so many years, we do not know the needs and desires of others. My mission is one of discovery and little more right now."

Ammudien's story confused Feigh. It was highly unusual for a new vendor to come to town without samples or supplies to advertise with. And, Ammudien's comment about 'simple enchantments' also caught his ear. Feigh opted to ignore the lack of samples but press the visitor more on other areas of interest.

"Enchanted goods? I thought the sale or possession of magical items was forbidden?" the human guard captain asked his gnome suspect, knowing good and well that no such ban had been placed on any such items and that the only reason they were rare was that they were typically very expensive to acquire.

"There is no such ban in Mechii or the other towns that I have visited," Ammudien cautiously replied, not very sure what Feigh's newest line of question meant for him. "If Tyleco does not allow enchanted goods, then we can either sell non-enchanted goods or simply pass by Tyleco in our trade route, but I was given to believe that we would be allowed to market those goods here as well."

Ammudien's answer was right. Enchanted goods could be and were commonly sold openly in Tyleco's market. This was something Feigh was very familiar with, but he was just curious to see how the gnome would respond to such an accusation. Ammudien's response could not have been more perfect, further disrupting Feigh's attempts to uncover a conspiracy.

But Feigh had one last avenue of questioning for the gnome.

"And how does your family enchant these items, which I assume are done for a fee? I suspect you ask your buyers to pay for the jewelry in advance to cover your costs and then purchase the enchantments?"

Feigh had hoped to glean something from the gnome's response here. After everything else, Feigh was confident that the gnome was pushing a scam where they asked people to pay in advance for enchanted goods that were either never delivered or never enchanted. If the gnome answered yes to this last question, then Feigh knew he was dealing with a charlatan and would very publicly run the would-be gnome merchant out of town.

"Actually, no, we do not accept payments in advance," the wise gnome answered, knowing what Feigh's poorly hidden intent was with the question.

"To the contrary," Ammudien continued, "we only accept payment upon delivery and confirmed satisfaction. Through our high standards, my family was able to secure exclusive production rights with the guild in years past. Those standards are something that we hold on to dearly, even now. We want our customers to know that our family and our business can be trusted, and taking money for things before they are provided does not symbolize trust in our family."

Ammudien paused for a moment to let that sink in with Feigh before continuing.

"And, to your question of the source of our enchantments, we do not require the services of a third party. Surely, someone of your position has noticed my different attire compared to most gnomish merchants that grace your city's market. My attire is that of someone who is skilled in the art of enchanting. I studied enchanting at the guild in Mechii for the sole purpose of continuing my family's trade. My brother and father are the jewel crafters while I am the enchanter. They make the pretty accessories while I imbue them with the various gifts our customers desire. The only thing we do not do within the family is mine the various ores and gems themselves. For that, we, like everyone else in Corsallis, go to the dwarves to purchase our raw goods."

Once more, Feigh's questioning was thwarted by the crafty gnome's answers. The captain of the guard was out of options and had little choice but to accept Ammudien's story.

"Well," Captain Feigh started, "while that seems odd compared to how most merchants operate, I can find little fault in that logic and have no cause to detain you longer—"

"Does this mean that I will be able to get an audience with your Lord Veyron?" an excited Ammudien asked before Feigh could finish his statement.

"Ahh, yes, Lord Veyron. I was just coming to that," Feigh answered in a tone that Ammudien immediately recognized as denial. "Lord Veyron is a very busy man, obviously, so he does not usually take audiences from merchants. His advisors manage Lord Veyron's purchases and screen any prospective goods to be sold to the high house of Veyron. At best, I can ask his advisors if they would be willing to meet with you to discuss your family's potential goods, but I'm quite certain that a personal audience with Lord Veyron himself is out of the question."

Ammudien's heart sank with Feigh's answer. Until now, their plan had depended on Rory's standing with the guard to get them both an audience, but it seems their faith in Rory's exalted status was misplaced. Nevertheless, Ammudien still had another plan to gain access to Lord Veyron.

"That would be most excellent if you could coordinate such a meeting. I understand that the running of a city as grand and as large as Tyleco must put a great strain on Lord Veyron's time. I would gladly meet with his advisors as a next best substitute to the actual man himself," Ammudien quickly said, accepting Feigh's offer.

"Please, wait here while I try to get you an audience," responded a somewhat dejected Feigh.

Feigh was certain that he would catch the gnome in a lie, but instead, it seemed that the gnome had turned the tables on him as he was now working for the gnome's interests and not his own. He struggled to understand how that had happened, but he had made the offer so now he was obligated to fulfill it as he exited his office on his way to go find Lord Veyron's advisors.

Chapter 4

"Hey, Rio, did I tell you about my encounter with Izu?" Nordahs asked his friend as the three elves continued their rapid but effortless sprint toward Rishdel.

"No, I don't believe you did," answered Riorik, a bit skeptical of his friend's claim, despite his own unknown encounter with the great forest spirit near the river's water just outside Rishdel, following his guild hunt.

"Wait!" exclaimed Kirin. "You think you saw Izu? Don't you two know that there are no spirit animals? Those stories are just fairytales."

"Right," answered Nordahs, obviously offended by Kirin's disbelief. "They are just as fictional as the Ascension Armor."

Nordahs' fiery response instantly put Kirin in his place. For years, it had long been thought that the stories about the missing armor were just tall tales that were more myth than truth. But now, they all knew the armor was very real. And if the armor was real, then perhaps Izu and the other spirits were equally real.

"I'm sorry," Kirin quickly apologized. "You are right. The armor is real, this cannot be questioned any longer. It's just that I have traveled all around these lands and never encountered a single great spirit."

"Not that you know," replied Nordahs. "Izu appeared like any other bear. There was no mystical glow or eerie fog that trailed behind his feet to show that he was somehow different from any other animal in the forest. It was only through observing his actions did I understand that I was in the presence of Izu. It is possible that many of us saw Izu but just mistook him for any old bear, and not a great forest spirit. Sure, he was bigger than most bears I had seen, but he was by no means gargantuan in size so that it was obvious."

"Well, what was so odd about his actions?" asked Kirin, still curious about Nordahs' claim.

For the first time since his hunt, Nordahs told Riorik and Kirin the truth about how he returned with his prizes. He described in detail about how he had stalked the strange bear through the forest only to always be spotted and to have his attempts to bag the bear thwarted. Nordahs talked at length about the bear's uncanny ability to know his exact location, even when the bear was in the cave and could not possibly have seen Nordahs' movements in the trees. The elf described the fight with the wolves and how Izu seemingly appeared out of nowhere to protect and defend the elf from the savage wolves. And finally, he talked about the exchange he shared with the bear, where it sat across from him and growled at the bow before walking away.

It was this last exchange that reminded Riorik of his encounter with a similar bear near the river.

"You know," Riorik started. "I think I may have seen Izu too."

This admission instantly got the attention of the other two elves, who quickly came to a stop and stared quizzically at Riorik.

"What do you mean, you 'may have seen Izu too'?" questioned a stunned Nordahs.

Riorik recounted his story of returning to Rishdel only to be distracted by a bear oddly playing in the river's water and how the bear seemed to call out to Riorik, wanting the elf to come to the water too. Riorik talked about how odd the bear's behavior seemed at the time and that he had discounted it on behalf of his own exhaustion from the hunt.

Nordahs felt a new level of kinship with his friend in their shared sighting of a legendary spirit like Izu. Over the weeks and months that had passed since his encounter, Nordahs had at times questioned his own sanity and the accuracy of his memory. There were days where he doubted the truth of his experience, but now, with Riorik's experience, Nordahs felt a new sense of reassurance that he was not crazy after all.

But Kirin, on the other hand, remained unconvinced.

"Oh, the two of you are certainly a pair, aren't you?" the brother said. "Just because you both see bears behaving oddly you both think you saw Izu. Nordahs' story might seem plausible to those who believe it, something I'm not sure I do just yet, but Riorik, your story seems like you just stumbled across a cub playing in the water, and you are making connections to Nordahs' story where there really aren't any. It just all seems a bit too convenient for me."

"Look," started Nordahs, who was growing annoyed with Kirin's disbelief, "I didn't ask you to believe me or in Izu. I simply asked Riorik, not you, if I had told him about it. If you want to think I'm crazy or that Riorik is grasping at straws to connect his experience with mine, then you are certainly free to do so, but do not attempt to convince me of what I saw because I'm the one who was there, who saw it, and lived it, not you. And maybe your lack of belief is why Izu hasn't revealed himself to you. Have you ever stopped to think about that?"

Nordahs' tone made it obvious to Kirin that this was not something he needed to push. The elven wizard put up his hands in surrender and slowly shook his head to signify that he would no longer question their claims or beliefs.

"Again, my apologies," Kirin said aloud to the pair. "This has all just been a lot to take in, so I find myself trying to draw the line of what I can accept and what I cannot. I mean, first, my missing father reveals himself to me. Then, I discover that the Ascension Armor is real, and the stories of its power are true. Next, I find that my only brother also knows of the armor and has found some for himself. And finally, that

our father apparently wants the armor to wage a war that would see

hundreds, maybe thousands, dead. It's just a lot to take in, and now you

two are talking about the existence of a magical spirit that protects the

forest. I don't know how much more I can take."

Riorik quickly hugged his distraught brother.

"It's okay, Kirin. I have struggled too, but that doesn't mean

that there is nothing left for us to uncover. We must keep an open

mind if we are to prevent the genocide our father plans. Besides, we

don't know that whatever evil grips his heart can't be repelled and our

true father finally returned to us. We need to accept what we see, not

what others want us to think, and we must trust one another in a time

where trust is lacking everywhere. If we falter, then there is no hope

and our father's war will spread here, to our home, to our mother's

doorstep. Would you lose our mother because of a lack of faith?"

Kirin listened to his brother's words and for the first time

thought of Riorik as a mature elf and not just his little brother. The

wizard was somewhat surprised by the articulate and profound words.

It was then that Kirin realized Riorik possessed the same skills that had made their father such a great leader. He had the ability to inspire hope and to ignite the flames of loyalty deep from within. Kirin began to feel that there was hope in their mission and that Riorik was the leader that the others thought him to be.

"You're right, Rio," Kirin said with a smile as he pulled away from his brother so that he could look him in the eyes.

Kirin beamed with pride as he looked into Riorik's eyes.

"There is much left for us to see and accomplish, none of which we can do standing here. You have opened my eyes and my mind to the mysteries left to uncover and to the hope of what we can save. You are the Ranger that our father would have wanted you to be and the Ranger I could never have been. Where you lead, I will follow."

The two brothers embraced once more before turning to Nordahs and indicating that they were ready once more to continue on their path home and to the uncertainty of the future ahead.

***

"What are your commands, sir?" asked one of Lord Shiron's generals once everyone had gathered in Kern's war room.

The room was small, cramped, and dimly lit. The walls were largely barren, with no decorations and only a few candleholders dotted around the perimeter. The center of the room was focused around a small table with an incredibly detailed model of the city and its nearby surroundings. It was the perfect planning piece to plan a siege defense, a close-by skirmish, or, as in this case, a precision escape from the city.

At the head of the table stood Lord Shiron himself, with the highest-ranking generals crowded as close to the table as possible. The lower-ranked officials were left to scrap and elbow for room behind the others as they struggled to see and hear what their leader's plans were for them and for the city.

"It seems that our beloved Kern is surrounded," Lord Shiron answered slowly. "To this, none can deny. Our purpose here is not to discuss that reality, but rather to form the foundations of a plan that will see to the safe withdrawal of the city's leaders and people of vital importance so that they may secure the future for the people of Kern."

Lord Shiron was intentionally being vague with his answer. The real point of this meeting of the minds was for him to order his soldiers to lay down their lives so that he could escape. Shiron had no desire to surrender his city with him in it, but Lord Shiron was a bit of a coward who did not wish to engage in a fight with a vastly larger army. He knew that if it came to war between the invaders and his army, that there was little hope of winning and that usually concluded with the death of the losing force's leader, which was Lord Shiron. Death was not something high on Lord Shiron's list of things to do, so he was inclined to get away with his head still firmly attached to his neck and air in his lungs.

But the leaders of Kern's army were not so easily fooled. Many caught the subtle message in Lord Shiron's speech. One even called it out for the rest who may have missed it.

"By 'the safe withdraw of the city's leaders and people of vital importance', you mean that you would like us to devise a plan to smuggle you out of the city while leaving the others here and subject to our inevitable occupier's whim and whimsy, right?" the annoyed military leader asked rather bluntly and loudly.

"Well," Lord Shiron said with a tone of arrogance, appalled in the face of his obvious failure at deceit, "the intent is for a select few of you to accompany me, and the rest of the noble family, out of the city so that we may garner support from others to take back our city while the rest of you remain here and hold out as long as possible. Our city's occupation will be in your hands, and I have the fullest faith that you, my most trusted generals, can and will protect our city while I humble myself before others in order to win their favor and aid."

He hoped painting a picture of himself bowing before someone else to protect and help his people might encourage his men to stay and fight. The plan did not go as expected.

"So, you expect us to stay here and die while you run off to dine and talk?" another general blurted out.

"Just how many of us do you plan to take with you, and how many do you plan to abandon?" another shouted.

It was quickly becoming apparent to Lord Shiron that his loyal subjects were not as blinded with loyalty as he had hoped. But of course, when faced with one's own mortality, it was only human nature to fight for one's own life before fighting for the life of another. There was little difference between their own desires to live and Lord Shiron's desire. The key difference was Lord Shiron's willingness without regret to sacrifice as many other lives as necessary to secure his own.

"Order! I demand order!" Lord Shiron shouted as he reminded the others in the room of their station in respect to his.

The rumble of shouts and talking quickly quieted as all eyes turned once more to Lord Shiron. He knew he only had one more chance at this and that if he did not choose his words carefully, then escaping the city would be the least of concerns. There was brewing all the signs of a rebellion in that very room, and one wrong word would mean Lord Shiron would not escape the room, much less the city.

"All of you, calm down this instant and remember your rank," he demanded. "You are generals of the Kern army and leaders of men. You are meant to have courage under these conditions, and your duty calls for my outright protection, does it not?"

He looked around the room as many of the military men hung their heads in shame as they nodded in agreement. Lord Shiron was right. The men had sworn an oath to protect their lord at any and all cost. Their lives were forfeit if it meant his survival. The overwhelming situation had caused them to all lose sight of that oath they had now been so shamefully reminded of.

"If this invading force should take the city, then my family and I are undoubtedly going to be killed. As are many of you, if not all. It is warfare basics to snuff out any leaders who may attempt to subvert or conspire against an occupying force, and that means all of us in this room today. This means that if any of us want to have a chance at life later, then some of us will have to stay and fight while others seek help. Given my position, I can best serve by bargaining with the nobles of the other cities to gain their support, and those who travel with me will use their knowledge of our city and our potential occupiers to lead whatever aid we acquire back here to help those who remain. We leave Kern not in cowardice but as part of a two-pronged plan to defend our city. Should one plan fail, the other plan may yet succeed, and countless lives could be spared. It will be dangerous, and some may die, but is that not a risk you are willing to take when you pledged to serve in the army?"

Lord Shiron's words burned in the ears of his generals. None of them doubted that occupation of the city was inevitable, regardless of any defense they mounted. It was more of a question of how long could they hold out against the invaders and at what cost. And, as much as none of them wanted to admit it, if there was to be a chance for success, Shiron's plan to seek help from other towns was necessary.

"What about sending birds for help?" one general standing opposite Lord Shiron casually asked. "If we are to stand a chance at defending the city, then we will need all the hands we can get, and those hands will need leadership. If we send a detachment with you, then that weakens the city's defenses, not to mention that it will take longer to walk to a city than it would a bird to fly there."

"I have been hesitant to send messages via bird," Lord Shiron replied.

His pride did not easily allow him to admit that he needed help from anyone else, but he dared not admit that to the men in this room. Instead, he opted for a more political answer.

"There is much distrust among the extended members of my family, as they all try to claim my rightful position as heir to the throne. An impersonal plea via a bird would surely go unanswered and viewed as an elaborate ruse or something. Only a personal visit has a chance of success. But, if it eases your concerns and any concerns of others in the room, then I will agree to send messenger birds out at the same time as my departure."

"When does my lord wish to depart and how?" the general nearest Lord Shiron sheepishly asked, as he capitulated and once more offered his service to his liege.

"Under the cover of darkness and through the southern tunnels is the most obvious exit, given our enemy's current position. Wouldn't you all agree?" Lord Shiron asked.

His question was met with various nods and words of agreement. Nobody in the room could think of a better option. The tunnels had been dug out many years ago, under the town's tall keep near the city's westernmost wall, nearest the steep cliffs leading down to the sea. It was the most fortified area of the city and the most obvious place to have such escape routes in case of war or rebellion.

"But what about the invaders? They expect an answer regarding your surrender before nightfall."

"We stall them," replied another general. "We simply tell them that the terms of surrender are being prepared and that we simply require a bit more time. If we make them think that surrender is coming, then perhaps they will wait while we ready ourselves against an onslaught."

After a few more minutes of discussing and organizing, Lord Shiron had selected three generals to travel with him and had given them orders to each pick two soldiers to come along as the group's guards. The others plotted the city's defense, and before long, a complete plan was set.

***

"My Lord, your deadline approaches but Kern has not complied. Should we prepare to attack?" asked the dark king's dark elf general as the two stood side by side at the edge of Cyrel's command tent, surveying the open and empty lands between their position and the gate of Kern.

The King of the North turned to his commander and looked his elven colleague in the face without saying a word for several seconds.

"We must remain patient if our ruse is to succeed," he finally replied. "We want the people of Kern to believe that our intent is not to harm them so our occupation can begin peacefully. We do not want a drawn out fight here and now."

The armored king paused briefly before continuing, "But a deadline is a deadline. We must show them that we are serious, so no answer will warrant force."

The protected elf produced a small piece of parchment, some ink, and a quill from a small desk just inside his tent. He scribbled a brief message on the parchment that read, "A deadline is just that. Answer soon or more will follow." He rolled the note into a tight spiral and handed it to his companion.

"Have one of your archers affix this to an arrow with instructions to place it firmly in the chest of a guard. That will show them that I am not to be ignored or taken lightly," Macadre's leader ordered.

With a click of his heels and a quick, shallow bow, the dark elf general took the note and headed off to find an archer to entrust with such a task.

A few minutes later, a loud cheer could be heard from the invading troops as they watched the arrow fly with expert precision before impaling itself through the soft leather tunic and deep inside the ribs of a guard sitting atop the wall surrounding Kern. The force of impact was enough to knock the unsuspecting guard from his feet, which sparked a flurry of activity around him along the wall.

The guards on the top of Kern raised their fists in anger at their attackers. It did not take long for them to find the note and understand its meaning. It was an ominous moment for the besieged guards, who had just been given orders to prepare to fight. There had been many doubts and questions among the city's guards and soldiers about what was to come, but now it was all too obvious, and it was certainly the last scenario any of them wanted.

Several minutes passed as the two armies watched one another with careful eyes to see what each's next move would be.

The city of Kern moved first.

The large iron portcullis that blocked the northern gate out of the city slowly raised before the heavy, thick wooden gate opened to reveal a single horse and rider. The rider sat tall in his saddle with one hand gripping the reigns and the other holding a flagpole with a large white flag flapping in the wind. The rider nudged his horse as the pair started a slow trot toward their aggressors.

With a simple wave of his finger, a warg rider eagerly hopped on top of his hairy, over-sized, wolf-like mount and rode out to meet their guest.

"I am here to offer the terms of surrender to your master," the guard told the warg rider, all while trying to control his very nervous horse, who was agitated by the presence of the large, snarling warg.

"This way," the dark elf rider replied, as he pulled on the long strands of warg hair he used to control the beast under him.

The dark elf rider led his human counterpart through the troops, going slow to ensure the human had ample opportunity to see just how massive their army was and to understand exactly what Kern would be up against should it come to a fight. The guard from Kern looked around with his wide eyes open. Their forces easily were double, if not triple, the number of soldiers behind Kern's walls. He struggled to contain his fear.

Their slow pace meant the pair did not reach the dark elf's leader's position for a couple of minutes, but the pair did eventually arrive, coming to a halt a few feet away from the armored king and his personal guards that largely stood between him and the horseman.

The guard from Kern slowly lowered the flag before dismounting from his saddle. He carefully stood with his hands stretched high above his head as he slowly turned in a circle to show that he was completely unarmed, exactly as requested.

"You've come prepared and authorized to offer your city's surrender and complete loyalty to me?" the masked king asked of his guest.

"I've come prepared to offer you a compromise," the guard shakily replied.

Instantly, one of the leader's guards readied his sword and quickly moved to strike down the human for his perceived insolence. However, before his sword could be bathed in the blood of the guard, he was stopped by the voice of his master.

"Wait! Do not kill him yet. Let us hear the young man out. Perhaps he has something of use to say," Nectana's sovereign barked at his guard.

The frightened guard let out an anxious sigh of relief that he had been given a reprieve from death.

"I've come to inform you that Lord Shiron has no desire to surrender, but rather plans to flee the city during your assault. We, the guards, vowed to protect the city, and we feel its protection is best suited by negotiating a peaceful surrender and transition instead of the unnecessary bloodshed that will undoubtedly end with the same occupation of our city. I am here to offer our submission to your will in exchange for your promise to allow us to continue to exist in our homes in peace. And to show the seriousness of this offer, we bring information about Lord Shiron's cowardly escape route as a sign of good faith."

The dark army's leader weighed the guard's offer. It was certainly appealing to the elf. He had hoped to take Kern without much fight, and if this guard's offer was true, then he would achieve that goal. But, he wondered if the guard could be trusted.

"Let's say I believe you and this is not some trick. How do I know your offer is true?" he asked the lone guard of Kern.

"Once the deadline passes, which is just a short time from now, send a few men toward the gate. You will meet little resistance, and what resistance you do encounter is more for show than anything else. Lord Shiron thinks that once night begins to fall and the fight rages between your forces and ours, he will be able to safely slink away out of the city through a secret tunnel. If you agree to spare us and our homes, I can tell you where the tunnel exits so that you may capture the coward and do with him as you please."

The guard's admission of a secret tunnel leading out of the city was new information to the invaders. No secret tunnels had been discussed by any of their spies leading up to the invasion. Everyone involved thought they knew all there was to know about Kern and their other targets, so this revelation was a bit of a surprise to all who heard it. This was something that certainly warranted more investigation.

"A secret tunnel, you say?" the lead elf asked as the human nodded in confirmation.

"How about this," the army's leader started. "You will give me the information about this secret tunnel, and we will partake in your façade of a fight to draw out your cowardly Lord Shiron. If my troops confirm your information and we capture him, then I will honor your wishes to be a benevolent occupier. But if your information proves false, the lives of everyone in Kern are forfeit and I will see that you all die painful and agonizing deaths. If your vows to protect the citizens of your city are true, then you will see to it to tell me the truth here and now."

"My vows and information are both absolute," the guard reaffirmed. "And I will eagerly provide you with the information regarding Lord Shiron's planned escape if it means protecting my city's future."

The guard asked for something to draw with or on. He was led just inside the large tent, where he was given a piece of parchment and ink. The human guard, whom some would later refer to as a traitor, wasted no time in drawing a rough sketch of Kern before marking the exit of the southern tunnel leading away from the city's keep.

The tunnel's exit was far to the east of the southern exit, too far from the gnolls still encamped there to assume that they would detect the escape on their own. As the light faded in the horizon, the deadline was upon them. If the peaceful occupation of Kern was going to succeed, word needed to be sent to the gnolls immediately so that they could reposition themselves to ambush the fleeing nobleman.

Once more, the warg rider was called. He was given the crude map and told to deliver it to the gnolls with instructions to hurry to the tunnel's exit. Their goal was the capture of Lord Shiron, but anyone else in his entourage was expendable.

The dark elf warg rider bowed as he accepted his latest commission. He shoved the rolled-up parchment under his belt before gracefully leaping onto the back of his hairy mount. He kicked the beast with his heels as he yanked on the hairy reins. The pair bolted away toward their target.

"Now, return to your post and let them know your offer has been accepted. A small detachment of my troops will be informed and dispatched to the city gates shortly to begin our faux fight. If your defense is more than you have said, then I will see the city razed to the ground. If Lord Shiron escapes by any other means, then I will reduce the walls to rubble before my troops slaughter every soul that dwells in your beloved town. And, having seen my troops up close, I trust you know the sincerity of my words."

"I do. And you will find that my words are sincere as well," the frightened guard insisted as he gingerly mounted his horse before spurring it to a gallop as he exited the enemy's territory.

Chapter 5

Bells rang out around the city as the guards posted on the wall

encompassing Kern shouted out warnings of the small detachment of

enemy soldiers advanced toward the city. The streets were filled with

people as they scurried about once again. The silence since the

morning's attacks had left some feeling complacent enough to try and

go about their daily routines, but the new threat that approached sent

them hurrying back to their homes and hiding places. Many people ran

to the church for sanctuary. Some ran toward the keep, only to find the doors barred shut from within. Others cowered in their homes, entire families huddled together wondering if today would be their last. For most, there was nothing to do but wait.

The sound of swords clanging together and the shouts of soldiers fighting could be heard echoing across the open plains just outside the city gate that remained slightly open during the skirmish. A large brazier above the gate was lit. The burning signal was the sign the lookout in the keep had been waiting for. The light of the brazier meant that the fighting had started and now was the time for Lord Shiron's escape.

"My Lord, the fight is lit. It time for us to leave," the lookout exclaimed as he ran down the stairs from his lookout position and into the keep's basement, where Lord Shiron and the others waited.

Lord Shiron turned to the scout and placed a hand on the winded lookout's shoulder.

"Toby[3], I need you to do something else for me now," he told his loyal servant. "I need you to run ahead and scout a safe path for us. I trust the tunnel's exit to be clear, but I'm told that many troops

---

[3] Pronounced "Toe-be"

surround the city, so we may need to find an alternate route to safety. Now, hurry."

The exhausted scout nodded and said, "Yes, My Lord," before taking off down the tunnel and into the darkness within.

"Let the birds fly," Lord Shiron commanded as he turned to signal another of his servants. "We must make this distraction complete."

The new servant rushed upstairs to signal the town's bird keeper to release the messenger birds as planned. And within minutes, the sky was filled with several birds taking flight from the roof of the bird keeper's hut. The sound of several wings furiously flapping could be heard over the noise of the fight that raged on outside the town. The birds climbed higher and higher into the air as they flew in a westerly direction as they attempted to exit the city and head off to their destinations.

But before the birds could get far, one by one the birds began to fall from the sky before hitting the ground with a thud. The first bird fell so unexpectedly that the bird keeper was confused as to why. But as the other birds fell, the old man soon saw the arrows protruding from his beloved avian friends' bodies.

It was the archers who had been posted outside of town with orders to kill the birds. The expert marksmen did not fail in their mission. They had almost given up in their silent wait for the birds to fly, so this was a joyful occasion for them. Each bird was fired on only once, and each bird was deftly knocked from the sky, exactly as planned. Not a single bird was left alive, or even made it beyond the city's walls for that matter.

To many of the citizens who watched as the birds rained from the sky above back to the city streets, it represented their hopes for salvation. Their hopes, like the birds, lay dead before them. Little did they know of Lord Shiron's true intentions.

***

Toby rushed through the tunnel. It was narrow, cramped, and dark, but that did little to deter or slow the scout. Through cobwebs and rat droppings, the young, sandy-haired man pushed on toward the tunnel's exit. The last glimmers of light could be seen highlighting its ever-approaching end.

Gary Richardson

After a few minutes of sprinting through the darkness, and few close calls on the often wet and slippery surface, Toby emerged from the tunnel and into the grassy lowlands just outside of Kern. Off in the distance, he could see the silhouette of the mountains where the barbarians made their home. It was the nearest town that Toby thought they might safely reach, and if the stories about the barbarians' fighting capabilities were true, it was the town Toby wanted to reach the most.

The nervous young man quickly glanced around to check the area, but he dared not make a sound. He saw nothing, he heard nothing, he felt safe. Toby ducked his head back into the tunnel and shouted back toward the keep's inhabitants to tell them the coast was clear.

With his message delivered, Toby now moved to his next duty, scouting a safe path away from the city. He crouched down to minimize his form to help avoid being detected. While remaining crouched, Toby began moving through the cover of the growing shadows and terrain, leaving the city of Kern in his wake. He could only hope that Lord Shiron and the others would exit the tunnel and be able to follow his trail. Another in the party was an expert tracker, so Toby was confident

90

there would be little trouble, but he still felt a bit concerned about being separated from the others. If he or they had an issue, then there was little chance that one could help the other. But this was the risk Toby accepted when he volunteered for this duty.

It did not take long before Toby had slipped away in the darkness, which was lucky for him. The gnolls came rushing to the tunnel's position shortly after Toby's departure. Toby's scent was still fresh in the air, but the gnolls were more distracted by the noise coming from within the tunnel that their sensitive ears could now pick up.

The shaggy dog-like creatures moved quickly and quietly to set their new ambush. It only took a few seconds for each of the handfuls of gnolls to find sufficient cover between the bushes and shrubs that lined the wall and dotted the landscape near the exit. Once hidden, the gnolls sat silently waiting for their approaching prey.

***

As soon as Captain Feigh left the office, Ammudien wasted no time casting another invisibility spell that would engulf his small frame. Mere seconds later, the roughly drawn runes passed over the gnome, who faded away behind them until there was nothing left of him to see.

"If he won't take me to Lord Veyron, then I will simply invite myself in," the annoyed gnome thought to himself as he sneaked down the hallway and past several guards.

The mage's desire was to be given a willing audience with the town's protector and leader, but since Feigh did not deem Ammudien worthy of Veyron's presence, Ammudien figured he would just do it himself. The gnome's new plan was to march through the guardhouse, across the town of Tyleco, and into the throne room of Lord Veyron himself, all while remaining invisible. The crafty gnome knew the plan to be risky and that surprising Lord Veyron might cause an unwanted commotion, but in light of the evil that would eventually find its way to Tyleco, Ammudien felt there were little other choices.

The tiny mage contemplated going back for Rory but figured if the pair of them disappeared that it might make for a larger scene than if just he disappeared. Rory was already suspected of being a thief, so making him invisible would only serve to reinforce that assumption. Plus, if it were revealed that Ammudien had tried to help Rory, then Ammudien would undoubtedly be labeled as a conspirator before both of them were jailed or executed. The scheming mage felt it best to leave his new friend to defend himself while Ammudien tried to convince Lord Veyron to stand against the oncoming storm.

The stealthy gnome tiptoed past the many guards he encountered in the guardhouse but was stopped cold by the solid wooden door that stood between him and the town streets. Even if he were visible, it would be a fantastic feat for the small mage to open a door that size, much less to remain undetected while doing so. However, for his purpose, Ammudien needed to remain both undetected and invisible so there was little chance that he could open the door without using magic without giving up at least one of those traits. Ammudien had no choice but to wait for someone else to open the door and give him a chance to slip through.

Fortunately, his wait was brief. A pair of guards approached the door while deep in conversation. The first guard opened the door and stood there holding the door open so the other could pass through first as they continued to talk. Ammudien jumped at the opportunity before him and scrambled through the door and outside, with the guards being no wiser to his presence than they had been before.

Once outside, the invisible gnome walked down the cobblestone streets of Tyleco as he dodged other people walking around him. Even the occasional cart would roll down the street, forcing Ammudien to take evasive action to keep from getting run over since nobody knew he was there.

The city of Tyleco towered over the short gnome but still seemed small compared to the towering spires and grand buildings of Mechii. By comparison, Tyleco was dirty and dank, whereas Mechii glowed with the surging magic that seemed to ooze from every corner of the gnome's hometown. Undaunted by the over-sized human dwellings and bustling crowds that filled the endless streets, Ammudien continued to make his way toward the castle that sat atop a hill overlooking the rest of the city.

"Surely, that's where Lord Veyron is," Ammudien thought to himself. "At least, if I was Lord Veyron, that is where I would be."

The gnome's progress was slower than desired as he was continuously forced to duck and weave around the gaggles of people that filled the streets at his every turn. The light was fading so he expected the people to return home to eat dinner, sleep, or spend time with their families, but it seemed that the people of Tyleco never slept, ate, or had families. As the minutes passed and turned into a measure of over an hour, the streets appeared to be no less busy than they had been when he first stepped out of the guardhouse. Ammudien was baffled by the excessive activities of the town's residents. Nevertheless, he pressed on, determined to reach the town's castle.

Several minutes later, his next obstacle loomed before him. It was the gated entrance to Lord Veyron's castle home. The large gate was closed, as was the smaller individual-sized door cut into the gate. This posed another problem since he very well could not just walk up and knock on the door and expect to be welcomed inside.

At first, Ammudien contemplated the worst-case scenario of just having to wait there through the night and try to gain entrance in the morning when surely the gate or the door would be opened. Alternatively, he hoped that he might get lucky again as he had at the guardhouse and just have some unsuspecting person open the door for him. The invisible mage knew the odds of that happening twice were low, but that did not mean that he could not hope against the odds. But aside from those two plans, the usually crafty gnome struggled to come up with any other ideas on how to gain access to the castle without exposing himself.

But, as luck would have it, the least likely of scenarios happened right in front of the surprised gnome. Ammudien looked up with glee to see Captain Feigh exiting the door in the gate with what the gnome could only assume were Lord Veyron's advisors, who were being escorted in their finely crafted and colorful robes to meet with the gnomish merchant still thought to be waiting in his office.

The parade of advisors seemed to go on forever as Ammudien waited for his chance to sneak past them and through the guarded entranceway. Eventually, the observant mage spotted a gap between two of the posh and pampered advisors for him to dash through.

Finally, he was in Lord Veyron's castle. Now, all he had to do was find the leader of the town and convince him to send his army to fight an unknown foe, all on the word of a stranger who snuck his way into the castle.

***

Lord Shiron and his entourage slowly and cautiously emerged from the tunnel. Only a few rays of light could be seen peeking over the horizon, as the sky was painted purple before it faded into the black of night. The stillness of their surroundings lulled them into a confidence about their success. With the growing sensation of security among them, one by one the group stood up tall and began to walk away from the tunnel and into the open landscape.

As the last of Lord Veyron's group exited the tunnel, the two gnolls nearest the exit moved to block any attempt at retreat. In unison, the others knelt low to the ground and stalked their prey. There were more humans than gnolls, but not by much. With the element of surprise, the gnolls had almost assured a victory.

One gnoll intentionally snapped a twig to draw the group's attention toward him. With their backs to the other gnolls, the last two gnolls sprang from their hidden positions and attacked the soldiers nearest them. Their razor-sharp claws reached around the unsuspecting soldiers' throats, and in what looked like a single coordinated attack, both soldiers had their throats gashed open and copious amounts of blood gushed from their wide-open arteries.

The soldiers gasped in pain as both men clutched their wounds, but neither was successful in stopping the steady flow of blood. In only seconds, both men fell to the ground cold and pale due to the lack of blood. Their eyes closed slowly as their life forces faded away, leaving only corpses in their place.

This sent a shock among the group, who began jumping and scrambling in all directions. The ambush had caused the chaos the gnolls had wanted. All that was left was for the vicious beasts to kill everyone but Lord Shiron. They had been instructed to only capture the fleeing city leader and return him to their master.

In the darkness and chaos, it did not take long for the gnolls to accomplish the first part of their mission. One soldier ran back toward the tunnel, as expected, but found his path blocked by the two gnolls who had remained there. In unison, the two gnolls pounced on the terrified man. One gnoll sunk his teeth and claws into the soldier's poorly armored calves while the other attacked the one quivering arm that clutched a sword. The attack was quick and brutal. In no time, the gnolls had ripped the soldier's limbs from his torso before joining the fray. The dismembered soldier was left to scream and cry in pain and fear as his wounds bled out before his eventual and inevitable demise.

The gnolls used the ever-increasing darkness of night and the remaining shadows to hide from the humans and their poor low-light vision. The hairy beasts lunged from their hiding spots sporadically to launch a series of hit-and-run attacks. The gnolls would rush in, slash or bite their targets, and then flee back into the cover of night before the armed soldiers in the group could manage much of a defensive counterattack. The guerilla tactics worked well for the gnolls, and in only a short time, they had managed to dispatch all of Lord Shiron's guards and companions. This left only Lord Shiron, who found himself surrounded by the snapping jaws of his opponents.

"Don't kill me!" Lord Shiron pleaded with the gnolls. "I can offer you riches or anything you desire."

His attempts to bribe the gnolls fell flat. The gnolls knew that there was nothing Lord Shiron could offer them that their master could not take away through his vicious vengeance that would surely follow any betrayal.

"We are not going to kill you," the lead gnoll snarled back at Lord Shiron. "No, our master wants to speak with you and he needs you alive for that."

This sent an immediate sigh of relief through Lord Shiron. He did not want to suffer such an undignified death, as he saw it, at the teeth of such savage and uncouth beasts. But, at the same time, there was still much to be feared about the now impending meeting with their master. Would his escape attempt be met with discontent? Would his callousness about leaving the people of Kern to die so he may live earn him favor with the unknown invader? What his outcome would be, Lord Shiron wondered but did not know.

One of the gnolls behind the befuddled and shaken lord stood upright and walked right up to Lord Shiron's back before shoving the nobleman forward.

"Move," the gnoll growled as the group moved to return to the main group still positioned to the north of Kern's walls.

It was a long walk, especially as the group tried to avoid the fake skirmish near the northern gate, but after several minutes, the gnolls arrived at their master's tent with their prisoner in tow.

"We have brought you the coward human leader, just as you requested," the lead gnoll announced as they waited for their master to exit the tent.

"Excellent," his voice from within could be heard answering.

A few seconds later, the masked leader emerged from the tent. His breastplate glowed in the night. The glow of his sword inspired fear among those who followed him, so the sight of his glowing breastplate immediately sent shivers down the spine of all who witnessed it. Even

Lord Shiron was both impressed and made fearful by the armor's mysterious shine.

The gnolls retreated from their positions as their master approached Lord Shiron. They did not want the glow's light to touch them, fearful that it would harm them. Instead, the glowing light illuminated Lord Shiron's face as he now stood toe to toe with his captor.

"You would abandon your people and have them die in your name, rather than stand beside them and die with honor?" the self-appointed king of Narsdin accused Lord Shiron.

"The people of Kern would gladly lay down their lives to repel a scourge such as yourself while I seek help from the other towns. That is what a good leader would do and inspires his people to do," Lord Shiron arrogantly replied.

His captor only laughed at the human's response.

"'Gladly lay down their lives' and 'inspires his people', really? Would you like to know how glad or inspired your people were by your pitiful actions?" the elf asked his prisoner.

Lord Shiron did not answer. Instead, he stood still and stared directly into the elf's eyes that were barely visible behind the metal mask that covered his face. Shiron's lack of answer was fine, as it was more of a rhetorical question and the dark king had every intention of telling Lord Shiron the truth whether he wanted to hear it or not.

"How is it that my gnolls knew where to lie in wait for you, huh?" he asked Lord Shiron sarcastically. "Your own troops came to me and gladly ratted you out. They even drew me a map."

He held out his hand, and the gnoll quickly placed the map in his master's hand before backing away from the shiny elf. Lord Shiron looked at the map in disbelief. His ego had always led him to believe that he was a beloved leader and the people of Kern would do anything for him, but now that lie had been shattered and the truth was damning.

"And now you expect me to grovel at your feet and serve you?" Lord Shiron said defiantly. His anger about being betrayed by his troops was overruling his better judgment as he now began to show contempt toward his captor.

"Well, yes," was the invader's response. "It would make my occupation of Kern easier if everyone was of a like mind. While some of your troops have served you up to me, there may still be a contingent of soldiers loyal to you, or at least to Kern, who might resist our presence here. But, with your support, then we may sway them from any thoughts of violence and avoid any more unnecessary bloodshed."

"I'd rather die than help you," Lord Shiron snapped back at the proposition before spitting on the elf's mask in a final act of defiance.

"Very well, have it your way," the armored king said.

And just like that, two trolls grabbed each of Shiron's arms to hold him in place while another approached from the rear with a pike in hand. The troll bent down to Shiron's level and slowly thrust the pike into the human leader's lower spine and up into his ribcage. Lord Shiron yelled out in agonizing pain until the pike pierced his lungs and left him with no more breath to scream with. The pike's point burst out of the dead leader's chest just below his throat. Blood ran like a river from the wounds as it streamed from the end of the pole and from the silk shoes that covered Shiron's feet. A pool of blood and mud formed under Lord Shiron's lifeless body.

"Take my new prize to the front of the line. Plant it in the ground for all to see, and let it be known that I am now in control of Kern and that anyone caught resisting or conspiring against me will meet a similar fate," the glowing elf ordered the troll, who immediately,

and without a word, turned to see his master's will done.

Chapter 6

Once inside the castle, it did not take Ammudien long to find Lord Veyron's quarters. There were only a few guards to be seen, as it seemed to the observant gnome that security in general around Lord Veyron seemed very lax. At first, this was a surprise to the invisible mage, but then after considering that nobody in Tyleco knew of the growing threat beyond their walls, it all made a bit more sense. There was no urgent need for a lot of security around their leader, or at least not a need that anyone in the city aside from Ammudien and Rory knew of.

The wide open, unprotected hallway through the main section of the sprawling building led directly to the throne room. The doors to the room were open with only two guards positioned outside. Ammudien could see Lord Veyron pacing around the empty room alone. This was his chance, the gnome thought, as he strolled right past the unaware guards.

Ammudien crossed the width of the room and took up a position near the back of the room, behind the throne and in the shadows. He had no intentions of lifting the spell any sooner than was necessary, but a covert meeting just seemed to require an adequate hiding spot and Ammudien was content to play the part.

Once in position, he was ready to engage Lord Veyron.

"Pardon the intrusion, Lord Veyron," the gnome's voice whispered from the shadows as Lord Veyron passed nearby.

The startled ruler stopped in his tracks and began to fruitlessly search for the voice's source.

"Who dares to sneak into my throne room unannounced?" Lord Veyron demanded in a hushed tone.

"I mean you no harm but saw no other way to speak with you. My requests to gain an audience had gone rejected, but I bring a message of great importance that you need to hear straight away," the voice answered.

"If you mean me no harm, why do you hide in the shadows like an assassin?" Lord Veyron questioned.

"If I had simply stepped out and revealed myself, would you have welcomed me or tried to have me arrested?" countered the gnome.

"Fair point," Lord Veyron admitted as he began to slowly back away from the disembodied voice. "What message is it that you have for me?"

"I think it best to start with something easier to understand, as what you are about to hear is bigger than you, me, Tyleco, or anything else that you know," Ammudien told his curious audience.

"Then reveal yourself and say what needs to be said," responded Lord Veyron as he continued to slowly back away.

The room was silent for a moment, and then the strange voice spoke again, only this time behind the retreating Veyron. The realization that the hidden speaker had moved stunned the now frightened leader, who stood perfectly still in the middle of the room.

"Do you think I am a fool?" the voice asked rhetorically. "I see your attempts to subtly summon your guards. If I were to reveal myself, you would have me arrested as soon as you laid eyes on me. Nay, I will remain hidden to you until I have your full confidence and my continued freedom is secured."

"And how is it that you think that can be accomplished?" a slightly terrified Veyron asked without moving.

"Please, take a seat and only listen. I am confident that if you hear all that I have to say, then you will agree that my freedom is more valuable to your reign than is my imprisonment."

At Ammudien's invitation, Lord Veyron moved to his throne and took a seat. There was still much trepidation in his actions and emotions, given Ammudien's continued concealment.

"I am ready to hear you out," Lord Veyron said, hoping that Ammudien really did not mean him any harm.

"Great," Ammudien said, "but first I will need something. Or more accurately, someone."

"What trickery is this?" Lord Veyron asked suspiciously.

"No trickery," Ammudien answered. "But, as someone in my condition, I have heard and seen things within your city that others would like to have remained hidden. As such, I am aware that your previous guard captain, Rory Cooper, is currently being interrogated by your current guard captain—I believe his name is Feigh—and that Captain Feigh is accusing your previous captain about a theft of a certain shield."

"What of it?" Lord Veyron questioned curiously. "The evidence suggests that my former captain took from one of my storerooms an item that belongs to my family."

"Nay, the item that was taken was never your family's. How it ended up here I cannot say, but I know that specific item belonged to another."

"Are you calling me and my ancestors thieves?" Lord Veyron asked with an insulted tone.

"I am only here to speak the truth. I know not the truth of how the shield arrived in Tyleco, only that it does not belong here."

Lord Veyron now began to suspect that the mysterious voice was part of a plan by his cousin, Lord Shiron of Kern, to acquire the shield to help bolster his claim to the throne.

Over the years, the family members had all fought over who was the rightful heir, each with their own claims to the throne, and there had been many attempts by each to swipe various objects from the others that they claimed supported their claims. If someone could acquire several, or perhaps all, of those objects then the thought was that their claims would go unopposed. But, to date, not a single object had successfully been stolen and the debate raged on.

"And how does Rory Cooper factor into your 'truth'?" a suspicious Lord Veyron asked.

"Because what I am about to reveal to you will prove that man's innocence. My observations of Captain Feigh lead me to believe that he is not an honorable man, and I would be ashamed if I knew that an innocent man was punished for a crime he did not commit. You and I both know that Feigh recently left here and was returning to the guardhouse where Rory Cooper is currently being held. It is surely just a matter of time before Feigh sends Rory Cooper to be tortured for information he does not have. Send a messenger to retrieve Rory Cooper, and after he is brought here, I will show you the truth of the shield."

"And in the meantime?" Lord Veyron asked, still skeptical of the unseen voice.

"While we wait, I will tell you a story. It is one I am sure you have heard before, but it is important that you know the whole story before we proceed."

"This all sounds a bit fishy to me, but I'll indulge you," replied Lord Veyron. "Just allow me to go fetch one of my men to go summon Captain Cooper here."

"Please go ahead," was the voice's response.

The voice had moved again. It was now to the side of the throne. It sounded as if the source was standing right next to the seated Lord Veyron, even though there was nothing and nobody to be seen there.

A confused Lord Veyron quickly stood up from his seat and walked at a fast pace toward the door. He had originally planned to have his guard bring Rory to the throne room and then wait to arrest the hidden bandit, but the voice's close proximity to his throne had distracted his mind. When he reached the door, Lord Veyron only remembered to instruct the guard to go collect Rory from the guardhouse and return him there.

The guard jogged off, his armor clanking with each step, to fulfill his mission. Lord Veyron watched as the guard sped away before turning and walking back to his throne. His eyes nervously glanced around the room, trying to find any clues about the voice's source and current position. He was unable to spy a single clue and returned to his throne no closer to revealing the voice's identity.

"Rory Cooper will be here soon," a concerned Lord Veyron reported. "Please, tell me the story while we wait. I only pray that this story has a happy ending."

"The story's ending will be up to you," Ammudien said from behind his magic veil.

Ammudien then proceeded to tell the story of the Ascension Armor, from start to finish. He talked about how the armor was said to be buried with its owners and was never seen again. The gnome spoke about the stories of the armor giving its bearers enhanced abilities that would set them apart from others. The mage told the human, who was listening intently to his words, about everything except how the armor glowed. He intentionally left that part out for a reason.

As the invisible voice finished the story, Lord Veyron seemed agitated about listening to a story that he was already familiar with.

"And what does this have to do with anything? I already know all of this," he huffed at his mystery guest.

"All in good time. Once Rory Cooper arrives, I will show you something that you do not know. Please, be patient," Ammudien's voice urged.

A few brief minutes later, Rory Cooper stepped through the doorway and into the throne room. What seemed like an invisible force, but was really just Ammudien, closed the doors behind Rory, sealing the three people in the throne room. It made Lord Veyron even more nervous as he now began to suspect that he was surrounded by multiple unseen forces, perhaps even ghosts.

Ammudien moved close to a confused Rory and stood behind his human friend as he fumbled with the invisible pack's bindings that hid the shield around Rory's waist.

"Just stand still and listen. Do not say a word," Ammudien whispered to his friend.

With the invisible pack and shield in hand, Ammudien quietly moved to the center of the room so that he stood between Rory and Lord Veyron, who was still seated on his throne.

"What if I were to tell you that the shield Rory Cooper was accused of stealing was actually the legendary Shield of Sagrim? What if I could prove that Rory Cooper did not steal the shield?" the voice questioned aloud in the echoing chamber.

"And how would you do that?" a curious Lord Veyron asked in response.

"Easily. First, Rory Cooper could not have stolen the shield if he does not possess it. And secondly, what if there was one more property of the armor that I could demonstrate to you now to prove its provenance?"

"Hmm, indeed," Lord Veyron began, "if you can reveal the shield's whereabouts then it may prove Captain Cooper's innocence. But, what other property of the armor could you demonstrate?"

Lord Veyron looked in the direction the voice was last heard. He watched as glowing symbols began to appear in the air. The runes appeared to rain down sparks to the shiny granite stone floors before disappearing. As the sparks fell, a form started to take shape in their wake. Several seconds later, the sparks ceased, and in their place, stood a small, robed gnome gripping the missing shield in his tiny hands.

Lord Veyron gasped at the unexpected sight.

"As you can see," Ammudien started, "I am in possession of the shield, not Rory Cooper. Your guard captain is innocent of this crime. I took the shield as it is an heirloom of great importance to the gnomish people, and I needed to verify its identity. This is the Shield of Sagrim, but more importantly, it may now play a bigger part in all of our futures than you may yet know."

"That certainly looks like the shield that sat in my armory for generations," said Lord Veyron as he studied the object from afar. "But how does this prove that it is Sagrim's Shield?"

"Ahh," Ammudien replied, "are you familiar with the armor's glow? The story talked about the ore glowing in the absence of light, correct? Well, if you would kindly help Rory and I extinguish the light that fills this room, the shield will prove itself to you."

There was some consternation in Lord Veyron's willingness to comply with the gnome's odd request, but through the ordeal, there had been no animosity or violence suggested toward Lord Veyron by his unknown guest, so the curious human agreed to go along with the suggestion. Except, there was a problem. There was no way to make the throne room dark. The large windows could not be barricaded or blocked enough to filter out the light.

"Sadly," Lord Veyron said, fully aware of the problem with Ammudien's request, "I don't think we will be able to make this room dark. However, perhaps you and I could move to an adjoining room where the light is less pervasive."

He then turned his attention to Rory, who still stood near the closed doors of the throne room.

"Captain Cooper, I will see that the charges against you are removed and I will consider restoring your previous position once you and I have had a chance to talk more about your unexplained absence. But I do not think that your presence is necessary for this exhibition. I will ask that you stay here if you wish to remain free of the dungeon and would like to continue thoughts of returning home."

Rory nodded and bowed at his lord's demand.

Lord Veyron motioned for Ammudien to walk toward a door leading to a small room just off the throne room. It looked to be a storeroom where the items often needed to attend to Lord Veyron and his grand throne room were kept for easy access by his many attendants. The room was dark with not a single window to illuminate the space. The pair walked into the room and found the fit to be somewhat tight but not too cramped.

Lord Veyron stared at the shield. There was a slight, almost indiscernible glow emitting from the equipment, but there was still a good bit of light filling the space through the doorway. Ammudien recognized the faint glow's cause and immediately moved around the stationary human to close the door behind them.

In the complete darkness of the room, a blue glow began to spread out from the shield and fill the room with the soft glow that only a piece of the mythical Ascension Armor could. Lord Veyron stood gobsmacked by the revelation of the armor's true existence. The typically articulate leader of Tyleco found himself in that instant at a total loss of words.

Eventually, Lord Veyron found his voice and his words once more.

"All right. I believe that this is the Shield of Sagrim, the same shield that my family has protected and possessed for generations despite not knowing its true importance. But what does this have to do with your message of great importance that prompted you to sneak into my throne room?"

"Let us return to your throne room, and I will tell you why this shield is so important and why you must aid me in my mission," Ammudien cryptically answered.

The two returned to the throne room. Lord Veyron once more took his seat in the throne, while Ammudien moved to stand near Rory before the two friends approached closer to the throne.

"Rory, tell Lord Veyron what you witnessed near the oasis," Ammudien encouraged his friend. "And not the whitewashed version you told Feigh. Lord Veyron needs to understand the truth if he is to fully see the threat that looms over us all."

Rory stepped forward and began telling Lord Veyron all about how he had followed Wuffred out of town and into the desert. He admitted that he did not know at the time that Wuffred had stolen the shield but had since been made privy to the truth. Rory described in great detail the clash between the two forces at the oasis, Wuffred's death, and the near cataclysmic force that blasted everyone from the oasis. Rory took great efforts and chose his words carefully to describe Riorik, Nordahs, Ammudien, and even Wuffred as trustworthy individuals with only the noblest of intentions while doing all that he could to describe the collection of savages that made up the massive army that marched from the north.

While Rory was telling his story, Ammudien discreetly slid himself and the shield behind his much taller human ally. Using Rory as cover, Ammudien placed the shield back in the pack, cast his invisibility spell over the pack before returning to Rory's side and leaning the now hidden package against the human's leg.

When Rory finished talking, Ammudien gave Rory a subtle nudge to remind him of the obscured package resting on his side. Rory looked down at Ammudien to acknowledge the gnome's signal, and then Ammudien stepped forward and addressed his host once again.

"So, Lord Veyron," Ammudien said, "as you have heard, a large and powerful army heads this way, and while I am in possession of the shield, the leader of this terrible force possesses two pieces. A single piece can turn an enemy into a nightmare foe that is almost insurmountable, but an individual that holds two pieces will be an unstoppable storm of destruction upon these lands unless we can put together a response of equal power to defend ourselves against such a malevolent force."

"Captain Cooper," Lord Veyron started, as he addressed Rory with his previous title, "you said you saw this great and fearsome army marching south from the oasis like they were most likely headed to Kern, yes?"

"That is correct, Lord Veyron," Rory dutifully answered.

"I do not see the danger then, my small friend," Lord Veyron said as he looked back to Ammudien's position. "This army moves against my main competition for the throne. And it is as they say, 'the enemy of my enemy is my friend.' This so-called 'malevolent force' actually helps my cause if it conquers Kern. Shiron would most certainly not be considered the rightful heir if his city falls in battle."

"Yes," Ammudien countered, "but what if instead of defeating Kern, your cousin allies with this force and they use their combined might to remove you from your seat of power? Or, what if using the power of two armor pieces, this force overruns us all and then neither you or your cousins have a claim to the throne. This potential conquest of Kern may sound good now, but what if it is part of a bigger plan?

One would not march with so large a force as what Captain Cooper has seen if the intent is to only capture or conquer one town. Nay, there is a larger plot involved that most certainly jeopardizes us all."

"Be that as it may, I will not risk the safety of Tyleco or the lives of my men to defend someone as dishonorable as Shiron, who refuses to accept my rightful claim as king. I will send my agents to monitor this situation and if, and only if, I deem this so-called 'force' to be a threat to Tyleco will I stand against them. Until then, Captain Cooper, I restore your rank and title and expect you to resume your position while my new gnome friend, I will give you this one-time offer: leave Tyleco now and speak nothing of this conversation to anyone or spend your days rotting in a cell. I cannot have you spreading fear among my citizens and town, and now that you have exonerated Captain Cooper, you have implicated yourself in the theft of my shield, which will remain here with me regardless of your choice."

This conversation just took a turn for the worse, and this was not the outcome Ammudien had hoped for. However, it was certainly an outcome the gnome had planned for.

However, before Ammudien could enact his escape plan, Rory took a step in front of the short mage and addressed Lord Veyron.

"I am glad to know that my service and my innocence has compelled you to reinstate me to my previous position. However, I cannot in good conscience accept such a post if my lord is unwilling to help those in need. I took an oath to protect Tyleco and all who dwell within its walls, this is true, but knowing the horrors that march this way, I have to extend that oath to protect all who share this land and call Corsallis, not just Tyleco, home."

"And," he continued, "I am somewhat ashamed that such an honorable man as yourself, who claims to be the king of men, would sit idly by while your fellow men are slaughtered, just because they do not reside behind these walls or are known to support your claims. If you are truly the king of men, then I beseech you to act kingly and protect all men and not just those who cling to the fringes of your cloak."

His words very visibly infuriated the ruler of Tyleco. None in his council would dare speak to him in such a way. To have his guard captain refuse an order and call him a coward was more than Lord Veyron could tolerate. His shoulders heaved as the angered leader took big, deep breaths. His cheeks turned bright red as his blood boiled with rage at Rory's insolence.

"Guards!" yelled the mad lord as he stood from his seated position and glared at Rory.

The door burst open, and a few armed guards came charging in with weapons drawn toward Rory and Ammudien.

However, Rory had once again unwittingly provided just enough of a distraction for Ammudien to ready another spell.

"Hold on," the mage told his friend as Ammudien reached out and grabbed the leather belt wrapped around Rory's waist.

Ammudien gave his wand a quick jerk up, and the runes that he had drawn on the ground around them sunk below the dark stone floor before the entire slab of rock lifted from the ground and levitated inches from its previous placement.

The guards stood and watched in a confused stupor. For many of them, this was the first magical experience they had witnessed, and it caused them to pause. Even Lord Veyron looked on with a shocked expression, not having realized that the gnome was obviously a magic caster before now.

"Do you have the shield?" Ammudien asked Rory, who nodded and patted the invisible satchel that he now gripped in his hand.

123

"Good," replied Ammudien before flicking his wrist forward and toward the large stained-glass window behind Lord Veyron's throne.

The floating stone began to move toward the brightly colored mosaic window, slowly at first but gaining speed as it moved. With each second, the stone also rose higher and higher from the floor until it was near the center of the glass. Ammudien and Rory covered up in anticipation of the inevitable collision. The front of the fast-moving stone smashed through the glass, sending shards of colored glass crashing to the ground behind them and Lord Veyron and his guards running for cover.

The slab and its occupants soared over the town and the wall that surrounded it before Ammudien's spell faded and the rock descended back to the ground. It was anything but a graceful landing, but the pair managed to avoid any serious injuries as they were tossed from the rock upon impact, and both rolled to a stop several feet away.

"Well, that was not exactly how I had expected that to go," Ammudien said as he stood up and began to brush the dirt and leaves from his robes.

Rory remained silent. The guard captain had sat down on the ground but said nothing. Ammudien, fearing the worst, rushed to his friend's side.

"Rory, are you okay?" he asked as he approached.

"No," Rory answered somberly. "I had expected better from Lord Veyron. He always seemed like an honorable man who was just in a bad situation due to the constant fighting over the throne. I always felt proud to serve him. But, thanks to you, he has revealed himself as no better than the kings of old who were less concerned with honor and providing for their kingdoms and more concerned with protecting only themselves and their power. There is no honor in letting others die without cause or hope. It should be the will of every leader to defend the defenseless from the threat of tyranny and to aid those who need it and would otherwise suffer without it."

Rory paused for a moment. He looked over at his friend, who was now sitting beside him and nodding in agreement with Rory's words.

"Just because there is no immediate threat to Tyleco doesn't mean that turning a blind eye to the plight of others is proper, or even sensible. I'm glad that we left and that we still have the shield because

Lord Veyron is certainly not worthy to wield it," Rory added as he clapped his hand over Ammudien's shoulder. "But now, where do we go from here?"

Chapter 7

Macadre's leader marched his army triumphantly through the gates of Kern with absolutely no resistance from the Kern army or the city's residents. He had occupied his forward base of operations with hardly any fighting, just as he had wanted. Now it was time to plan the next phase of his conquest.

The invaders wasted no time in taking control of the city's large keep and the barracks located nearby. He had instructed his army not to loot or pillage the city yet, as they needed their continued cooperation for the time being. The gnolls, trolls, orcs, dark elves, and humans that made up his army roamed the city streets but were careful not to damage anyone's property. For the residents of the city, many looked at the odd figures with a sense of terror and disgust but dared not scream. There were several doors and shutters closed as the outsiders approached, but not a single incident unfolded between the two groups.

So far, the occupation of Kern was a success and the transition of power had happened very smoothly.

The humans of the army even asked around to locate the merchants in town as they offered to buy goods from them to resupply the army's depleted stocks. Most had expected the invading force to simply take what they wanted, so the idea of them paying real money at fair prices for goods and services was most unexpected. Even the local blacksmiths had been summoned to the barracks where they were paid a fair wage to help mend and maintain the weapons and equipment that had not been serviced before everyone marched out of Macadre days before.

Some residents of Kern actually were so relieved by the civilized behavior of the invaders that they willingly helped them and even began to welcome them in Kern. Others, not so much. There was a contingent of residents that found the friendliness of the invaders to be just a bit too overzealous and were suspicious of the invaders. All of this, of course, was to be expected, and it did not take long for word to spread among their supporters that money would be paid to those who informed on those who resisted their presence. And within hours of their occupation, people of Kern started going missing if they spoke out against their new 'friends'.

*　*　*

Meanwhile, in the keep, the masked king met with his generals once more. Instead of crowding around his carved map of the continent, which had remained in Macadre, he had hung a large drawing of the area from the tapestries that adorned the walls of the room. The map was extremely detailed and appeared to be a high-quality copy of the carved map back home. The only difference was a series of small pins placed in the drawing that replaced the larger ornate tokens used on the table.

"Thanks to the quick and largely uneventful fall of Kern, we will be able to move on to our next targets sooner than expected and with a greater force than previously estimated," their leader boasted to start the meeting.

"I had expected more resistance from the leaders here, so we had estimated our losses to be at five percent, but thanks to the absolute cowardice and failure of that pitiful excuse of a would-be king, our losses were zero. In fact, I believe we have actually grown our ranks as some of the men in Kern's army have pledged their service to me, correct?" he said as he turned to look at one of his other commanders standing nearby.

The white-haired human with his scarred face and dark skin tones stepped forward after being addressed by his master.

"Yes, sire, we have received many offers of support from those who do not support the cowardly actions of their previous leader. If I had to put a number on it, I would say roughly half of the standing Kern army is ready to serve you," he answered.

"Should I have my squad leaders tell them to prepare to march on our next target?" the commander asked after a short pause.

"No," was his king's immediate and absolute answer. "I am still not convinced that their support is unflappable, and in the events ahead, I dare not risk that betrayal in the heat of battle. Tell them that they may best serve me by remaining here and staying vigilant against any threats of uprising or rebellion. In fact, find the highest-ranking soldier among them and promote him to the leader of my 'Kern reserves', and his orders are to secure Kern as a place of safe harbor for my men as we look to free others from the oppressive hand of their elitist leaders. Surely the naïve human will believe such a story while we are left free to conquer the other towns before teaching them the true meaning of misery."

A chorus of laughs broke out among the generals and commanders of the army as they thought of their lies to the people of Kern and the prospect of brutal torture and revenge on the races they all associated with the cause of their own miserable existences in the barren and harsh Narsdin region.

"Because of our success here at Kern," the masked leader said as the room began to quiet, "I have decided to escalate the timetable of our advance."

This quickly caught the attention of those still snickering and jesting at the previous sentiment. Now, the room was dead silent. Everyone simply stared at their master in surprise and wonder. Everyone was anxious, and at the same time nervous, to hear his new plan.

"Previously, the plan was to march city by city along the eastern edge of Corsallis before turning our attention to the humans who make their homes in the middle of the continent. Only after defeating those cities would we turn our full might on the snobbish elves of Rishdel," the armored elf began.

"But," he continued, "now I think it best to split our forces and take the towns of Dresdin, Mechii, and Rhorm in rapid succession. While one group attacks the halflings at Dresdin, the others will march on to the next targets, and then while a group is fighting the gnomes at Mechii, the last group will continue on to Rhorm. As one group completes its task, that group will march to the next target to offer aid if needed. Once all three groups are reunited at Rhorm, we will make our way to Fielboro to begin our assault on the humans."

"And how do you suggest we divide our troops to implement such a bold plan?" one of the dark elf generals asked, quite obviously concerned about the plan's ability to succeed.

"The halflings at Dresdin are not known to have much in the way of an army or even a strong city defense for that matter," the lead elf replied. "Those odd beings are mostly farmers who sit around eating their produce and smoking their pipes. They will offer little resistance and can be overrun with a small force of archers and wargs. The only reason we need to bother with them is to prevent them from alerting anyone else to our presence."

"And the dwarves, while stout and sturdy, tend to make their homes in the caves and tunnels of the mountains they endlessly mine for ore and gemstones. Those cramped caves may deter my larger orcs and trolls but are similar to what my dark elves, gnolls, and wargs are used to back home. We can clog the caves with boulders and force their numbers through choke points. That will reduce the power of their numbers while allowing my forces to inflict maximum damage both inside the caves and out."

"And what of the gnomes of Mechii and their magic?" asked another of his generals.

"The bulk of my forces will be centered there. I do not expect the gnomes to just give up as this pitiful human did, and their magic can be a major obstacle in any fight. Our best advantages here will be the element of surprise and superior numbers. Mechii has many buildings and residents scattered out in the open, so we will not be able to trap them like the dwarves. And, like the halflings, there is little in way of an exterior defense wall to protect the city, but I'm told by an insider that there are multiple magical protections in place around the city that may obstruct our advances. It will require that key structures be destroyed so that we may weaken their mystical protections before we can claim Mechii as our own."

"And you still think it wise to bypass Barbos?" asked one of the few gnoll commanders allowed in the meeting.

"The barbarian mercenaries of old are long gone. They are but merchants and seafarers now who take great strides to keep themselves separated from the rest of Corsallis. As long as we do not interfere with them, then I am certain they will not interfere with us. But, if a time comes that we need more fighters, they may yet be able to provide us with the extra force needed, for a price of course."

Little did the well-equipped elf know that his earlier campaigns in the area had already ruffled the feathers of the barbarians, who were now on the watch for more outsiders. Their beloved fighter Alaricea had been killed by his orcs, along with many of the men under her command, and now, the barbarians wanted revenge. Baolba and his small group had fled the area before reinforcements from Barbos could arrive, but that did little to quell the long-burning fire for vengeance that dwelled within every barbarian.

"The humans acted as expected in their attempts to send out messenger birds. My archers did a fine job of not letting that message get beyond the walls of Kern," the elf continued, totally unaware of Toby's escape from the tunnel. "Each city's assault forces will contain a contingent of archers to continue that approach of ensuring that no messages get out. If any city not already conquered gets word of our arrival beforehand, our plans will suffer and with it our people. The continued secrecy of our presence is paramount."

"You mentioned moving up the timetables," interrupted a young, dark-haired human. "When would you have us put this new plan into action?"

Their master's response was instantaneous and without hesitation of any kind.

"Immediately."

Again, the room fell silent as that answer was absorbed by those in the room. It should not have come as a surprise to them as their master's impatience was well known. If anything, it would have been a greater surprise if the answer was anything but immediately. Regardless, the commanders had fallen into a sense of complacency thanks to the easy victory and had hoped for a short rest before carrying on with the burdens of war, but it was not to be. The order was given, and now they were expected to carry it out.

A collective sigh could be heard from the disheartened military leaders who had hoped against hope that they would get a break. They each turned and filed out of the room and off to their respective groups to pass on what they had been told.

***

The three elves glided gracefully over the terrain and moved through the forest surrounding their destination with ease. Where many others would be required to move slowly or find alternate paths, the nimble elves casually moved around or over any such obstacles and carried on their way without a second thought. It was a gift that they had become accustomed to but had rarely been able to fully exploit while in the company of their other non-elven friends, so it was a welcome treat to move like elves once more. It made their trip to Rishdel much quicker than it would have been for anyone else, and it did not take much longer for them to see the thick wooden walls of their home than it did for Rory and Ammudien to reach Tyleco.

Unaware of the problems their friends had faced and unaware of what problems may wait for them here, Riorik, Nordahs, and Kirin pressed on and soon found themselves talking to the Rangers stationed at the gate guarding the main entrance to the elven village. But not before Riorik had removed the greaves that covered his legs and put the uncharacteristically flexible armor back deep in his pack and safely out of view.

"Halt!" yelled out one of the guards as the two Rangers drew their bowstrings and aimed at the unexpected arrivals.

"Don't fire!" yelled Riorik. "I am Riorik Leafwalker, this is my brother Kirin, and this is Nordahs Bladeleaf. We are residents of Rishdel."

"I know who you are," replied the Ranger sarcastically. "You and Ranger Bladeleaf have been gone for some time and feared dead. Kirin Leafwalker, aren't you supposed to be off studying magic with the gnomes?"

"I am. I mean, I was," answered Kirin, unsure of the Ranger's line of questioning. "But, as you can see, they are not dead, and we are all here now. We come with important news and must be allowed to speak with the guild elders immediately."

"Commander Greenblade will want to speak to the two of them first, I'm sure," responded the elven guard. "We will escort you all to the guild where he will hear what they have to say about their disappearance, and then he will decide who talks to the elders and about what. They may be given an audience to hear their punishment for desertion while you are sent back to Mechii."

The guard turned and shouted down to other guards behind the wall, "Open the gate!"

Riorik and the others could hear the sound of the massive timber log used to secure the gate scraping against the massive logs of the gate as the elves heaved to lift the enormous object from its restraints. It took several seconds for the huge log to be moved, followed by a loud thud as one end of the log was dropped to the ground while the elf pushed the gate open just enough for the three arrivals to shuffle through and into the village.

Once everyone was inside, the Rangers at the gate wasted no time in closing the gate and working to replace the gargantuan wooden lock back into place. The forest was full of beasts and animals that needed to be kept out of the village, and the village was still on high alert following the recent encounter with the gnolls and orcs just a few weeks before, so such security was no surprise to Riorik and the others who just watched the effort as if it was just an ordinary event, because for the elves of Rishdel it was.

After the gate was adequately locked, the order was given for the two guards who had operated the gate to escort the three new arrivals to the guild and to make their presence known to Commander Greenblade. The group casually strolled through the dark and empty streets of Rishdel toward the gigantic tree the Rangers guild called home. Riorik yearned to go see his mother and tell her all about his adventures but knew that would not be allowed until he talked with Commander Greenblade.

It had only been a short time since their last stroll down the street, but in light of all that they had seen and experienced since leaving Rishdel, this trip was like indulging in a succulent exotic desert to the two young Rangers. It was something they never expected to experience again when they first set out on their grand adventure and on many occasions since feared the only way they would return home was as corpses. But rather now they walked on their own two feet, breathed in the clean forest air with their lungs, and gazed on the revered forest that elves had called home for centuries with their own eyes. It was a bittersweet homecoming to the pair, who knew that if they did not succeed in getting support to fight against Cyrel's army that it might be the last time they ever see their beloved home.

In a few brief minutes, the group arrived at the carved double doors leading into the guild. A Ranger posted at the door opened one side and allowed the others to enter. One of the escorts told a Ranger seated just inside the door that Riorik and his companions needed to speak with Commander Greenblade. The seated Ranger advised the group to wait there while he went and fetched the commander. It was only a brief wait before the Ranger returned with Commander Greenblade following close behind.

"Well, I'll be," the commander blurted out at the sight of Riorik and Nordahs.

Commander Greenblade, recalling his orders for the two Rangers, quickly glanced around the room to see if Wuffred, or Hugh as the commander still knew him, was with them. He was relieved to not find the berserker's presence obvious but was curious to hear what the two elves had to say about their mission. The commander stared at Kirin too. He did not recognize the oddly dressed elf since Kirin had opted to study in Mechii and not with the Rangers.

"You two," Commander Greenblade said loudly to Riorik and Nordahs, "come with me. Your friend stays here though."

Riorik and Nordahs looked at one another, and then at Kirin. They all shrugged their shoulders before the two Rangers headed toward Commander Greenblade as ordered.

Looking at the two Rangers who had escorted the group here from the gate, Commander Greenblade gave them another order.

"You stay and keep watch on this one until I figure out what is going on."

The two Rangers saluted and acknowledged their orders before taking up positions on either side of Kirin. Kirin only looked at his guards with dismay and acceptance.

"To my chambers," Commander Greenblade directed Riorik and Nordahs as the trio of Rangers walked away.

***

141

"So," Commander Greenblade started, "tell me, did you complete your mission?"

The question was an obvious if not a subtle reference to his request for them to kill their friend.

"Yes," Riorik answered. "The berserker is dead, just as you ordered."

"Well, the pair of you have been gone for some time. I think an explanation is in order too," the commander pushed.

Riorik, not being a strong liar, wrestled with his thoughts on what to tell the commander. But before the stammering elf could think of a story, Nordahs spoke up.

"We led him far off into the forest, just as you wanted, but since he was still weak from his injuries, it took us longer than expected. As day turned to night, he kept urging us to return to the village, but we were trying to reassure him that it was fine, and we still had plenty of time to get back. We think he started to get suspicious shortly thereafter, so we tried to move quickly, but apparently not quick enough."

"The plan," Nordahs continued as Riorik just listened as intently as Commander Greenblade, "was for Rio—um, sorry—Riorik to distract him while I shot him through the heart with my bow from behind. We were both a little concerned about his abilities, so we wanted to keep as much distance between us and him when the moment came just in case."

"And how did your surprise attack go?" asked Commander Greenblade.

"It did not go as planned," answered Nordash before continuing his tale. "I had a full draw on my bow and was taking aim but just as I readied myself to take the shot, he moved. Instead of a clean shot through the heart, my arrow pierced his side at an angle and missed his heart. The point protruded from the front of the opposite side. I had to have punctured a lung, but the idea of an instant kill was lost."

"Yeah, yeah," Riorik interrupted as he tried to join in the story. "And he went mad. He was yelling and screaming in anger. All we could think to do was run, but we didn't want to run back here in case he chased us."

"Which is exactly what he did," added Nordahs, eager to build off of what Riorik had said. "We were forced to run through the night as an enraged berserker chased us relentlessly. I tried to stop and get another bow shot off a couple of times, but he was covering the distance between us too quick to safely attempt another shot in the dense woods."

"So," Riorik jumped back in, "we decided to try and lead him further away from the village and out into the openness of the plains near the human town. We figured that would give us a better shot to stop his rampage."

"Not to mention that if something happened to us that the proximity of the human towns might catch his attention, at which point he would be their problem and not yours," Nordahs was quick to add as he tried to give more legitimacy to Riorik's claim.

"That was some good thinking, put the berserker off on his own people and let'em do your dirty work. So, the humans actually killed him then?" Commander Greenblade asked as he thought he understood where their story was going.

"Quite the opposite actually," answered Nordahs.

"We all know that humans are nothing but liars and thieves, right?" he asked rhetorically, attempting to play off the racist stereotypes that had been passed down since the time of the great segregation that saw the races largely close their doors to each other.

Commander Greenblade silently nodded in agreement with Nordahs' suggestion.

"Well," Nordahs continued, "we emerged near a camp of these filthy humans. They saw us being chased by the berserker and immediately tried to come to his aid. They joined him in chasing us. At that point we felt we had two options, kill them all and risk starting a war between the elves and the humans or try to lose them all. We opted for the second choice. Thankfully, humans are pretty slow compared to us, and by this time the berserker's wounds were finally beginning to take a toll, slowing his pursuit down too. It did not take us long to escape our pursuers, but now we had lost our target as well."

"So, the berserker is still alive?" Commander Greenblade asked angrily.

"No, no, no," Riorik quickly answered. "He is dead, we just didn't kill him at that point. Right, Nord?"

"Right," answered Nordahs. "We knew the humans would take one of their own back to camp to treat any wounds, so we waited until the cover of night when the humans can't see very well, and we snuck into their camp while they all slept and slit Hugh's throat."

"What of the other humans? Did you kill them too?" a concerned Commander Greenblade questioned next.

"No. We left them alive, but we made it look like Hugh had been killed by one of their own by taking a human dagger that was left lying around in the camp and using that to slit his throat before leaving the bloody blade behind. We figured it best for them to think another human killed him than to suspect us or any other elves, since they had seen us fighting with him previously," Nordahs said casually.

"Yeah, we even grabbed some gold from their camp and put it in Hugh's pack so it would look like he was trying to steal from them so nobody would question his death too much," Riorik added.

Commander Greenblade was completely convinced by their story it seemed as he grinned with glee at the level of effort and stealth his two young Rangers described in completing their mission while hiding their actual level of involvement, even in such a close combat situation. Rangers were well known for their fighting abilities, but their stealth also made them ideal for assassinations, not that many had been conducted in recent years, and here sitting across from Commander Greenblade were two Rangers that seemed to excel at that deadly art. It filled the elf who had trained them with pride.

"So that explains a lot of the time that you two were gone and how you were able to complete your mission, good job by the way on that, but there is still some time unaccounted for that I need to understand. After you killed the berserker and framed the humans, excellent strategy on that too, why didn't the two of you immediately return to the guild?"

At this point, Nordahs was out of lies. It had taken all of his creative thinking to concoct that much of a story, so the newest line of questions left him scrambling for answers. But by this time, Riorik had gotten his creative juices flowing and was ready to take charge of their story.

"Well, we decided to wait through the night near the human campsite. We wanted to watch and see what happened when they discovered Hugh's body and make sure that they didn't make a move toward the forest. We felt it prudent to make sure that our plan worked and that no blame or animosity was directed at Rishdel or the Rangers."

"I see," replied Commander Greenblade, "That was good thinking. It is always prudent to make sure your target is down or that your mission is complete instead of just assuming it is and walking away. It would seem that I taught the two of you well."

Riorik and Nordahs exchanged a quick look at Commander Greenblade's last statement but were careful not to get caught.

"So, what happened then?" the intrigued commander questioned.

Riorik now decided to play off of Commander Greenblade's ego a bit more.

"Well, just as you taught us," he started, "we decided to take the opportunity to scout around and try to learn more about our surroundings and any potential threats."

Commander Greenblade beamed with pride as Riorik's words stroked his overinflated ego.

"And?" the commander asked, hoping to have his ego stroked even more.

"And that is when we saw the dark threat that loomed just beyond the border. We thought it best to closer inspect what we thought we saw, so we spent the next few days getting closer and closer to it, but once we had gotten close enough to see everything in full detail, we knew we needed to return to Rishdel at once and speak with the guild elders."

Riorik ominous and somewhat cryptic words caught their commander by surprise. He had been expecting them to tell about what they did based on his tutelage but instead, he heard about some 'dark threat'. He now looked at his recruits with a confused expression.

"What 'dark threat'?" he asked.

"Please, take us to the guild elders, and we will describe it to both of you then. Each minute we wait, the threat moves ever closer," Nordahs urged.

"Why did you not speak about this threat sooner?" Commander Greenblade barked in anger and confusion. "Why did you choose to sit here and regale me in the details of your mission and not of this threat?"

"You wanted to know what happened, so we figured it best to explain the whole story," Riorik answered in a very intimidated tone.

Commander Greenblade only growled at the pair before slamming his hands down on his desk and standing up.

"Come on!" he shouted before storming out of the room and toward the elder's meeting hall.

"Summon the elders!" he shouted to another elf as he flung the door to the meeting hall open.

"Sit!" he yelled at Riorik and Nordahs as he pointed to a couple of chairs in the middle of the room.

All three Rangers, Nordahs, Riorik, and Commander Greenblade, took their seats, and now all they could do was wait for the elders to assemble where they would finally get a chance to warn them of the threat that looms beyond the forest. Riorik and Nordahs were just glad that they made it this far without being arrested as traitors.

But, through it all, Riorik could not help but wonder what was happening with Kirin, who had been left at the guild's entrance.

Chapter 8

The guild elders slowly filled the meeting hall and looked down at the three Rangers seated in the hall's main floor through their groggy, sleepy eyes. Their pointed ears stood tall through the long, flowing white hair that all of the elders seemed to have. Their seats formed a half circle around the hall several feet above the floor.

Once the group had all taken their seats, the main elder elf, Elder Bostic, addressed Commander Greenblade.

"Commander, I understand that it was you that summoned us here at this late hour. Please explain."

The elf commander stood to address the elders, as was the tradition. His posture was straight and tall, just like a good soldier.

"These two elves were sent out to complete a mission that we had all agreed to, one regarding a certain human among our ranks," he started, making sure that the elders knew that they were the two tasked with killing the berserker, a task the elders had given Commander Greenblade.

"And upon completing their task," he made sure to emphasize that point for the elders, "these two Rangers spied a threat to Rishdel just beyond our borders and returned here to speak with you all about that threat. I summoned you here as they were adamant that you be informed immediately."

"And what kind of threat do they speak of?" asked on the elders, unconvinced that such a threat existed.

"I think it best to let them describe it for you as I do not fully know yet myself," the commander answered.

"You mean to tell us that you summoned us from our slumber and did not verify this so-called 'threat' first?" another of the elders asked angrily.

Commander Greenblade had been so enthralled with their story and his own self-importance that when the story changed from gratifying his ego to a word of warning, his emotions got the better of him. This was the first time that he had considered the fact that they were now in the elder's meeting hall and he had not even heard why he had summoned them. He began to doubt the validity of his actions and began to get angry with Riorik and Nordahs for the potential embarrassment they could cause him.

The lead elder, Elder Bostic, tapped his wooden staff on the floor to quell any conversation and to draw everyone's attention to him before he spoke.

"Regardless of whether or not Commander Greenblade has verified what these two Rangers want to tell us, we are all here now, so let us hear them out. It will be up to us to determine the validity of what they have to say, and if we think it was a waste of our time, then we will address that with Commander Greenblade then. But until such time, let us perform our functions and duties as elders."

Elder Bostic's word was law in Rishdel, and since he decreed that they should listen to Riorik and Nordahs, none of the other elders dared to defy or question him. The elders now all sat with their eyes now firmly fixed on Nordahs and Riorik in the center of the room.

The two friends exchanged a couple of nervous glances, unsure of where to go from here. They had planned to talk to the elders as part of their grand scheme, but neither of them had thought of what to say if they got that chance. Now though, they needed to get their act together and quick, before they lost the elders' interest.

Riorik nervously stood up to mimic what he had seen Commander Greenblade do earlier. He wanted to speak, and he wanted the elders to know that, but he was still unsure of what to say exactly. Nevertheless, he knew he had to say something.

"Oh, esteemed elders of the great Ranger Guild of Rishdel," he started, hoping to think of what else to say as he spoke, "I bring news of a grave threat that approaches. I stand here before you to warn you of impending doom if we do not act to stop this malicious force."

He stopped there, unsure of what to do next. Riorik's nerves were working against him. His mouth was dry and sweat dripped from his face. His hesitation was obvious, but his words had actually said very little.

"What exactly can you tell us about this threat that will doom us all? You have not said anything of value that would help us 'act' as you put it," one of the elders stated, pointing out the obvious omissions in Riorik's warning.

Riorik tried to answer but only managed to stutter and stammer like a fool in front of the elders. Nordahs watched his friend's failure and knew he needed to join in the conversation. He now stood up like Riorik as he saved his friend from the elder's question and claim.

"Riorik and I witnessed a large army marching south from the Narsdin region. After watching the group for some time, we surmised their goal is to start a war, a war that would find itself on our doorsteps if we do nothing to prevent it."

Many of the elders dismissed the elf's words.

"The Rangers of Rishdel have swatted away such attempts in the past with ease. All this talk of doom and gloom are surely exaggerated, and there is no need for such alarm," one of the elders boasted.

"I think you speak too soon," Nordahs replied to the elder's arrogance. "The army we saw was many times larger than any number of Rangers Rishdel has ever known. We would be grossly outnumbered in a fight against this terror."

Again, his claims were cast aside by the arrogance of several elders.

"Bah," one of them huffed. "The Rangers of Rishdel are often outnumbered, and yet we have always prevailed. Our history has proven time and time again that it is not the number of soldiers who fight that determines the winner but rather the skill and devotion those fighters display that allows one group to be triumphant over another. And the skill and devotion of Rishdel's Rangers are better than that of any possible foe."

"Do you remember the recent fight between the orcs and gnolls just outside of our gates?" Riorik asked, his tone dripping with sarcasm and anger at the elders' dismissive attitudes. "Well, we had the greater numbers in that fight and while we did come out victorious, our losses were greater than theirs. Not to mention that the only reason we won was that we had the help of a berserker that you all deemed unworthy and ordered us to kill."

His sharp, biting words got their attention, albeit their opinion of him was now somewhat lower than it already was given his relationship to the elven traitor Cyrel Leafwalker.

"The force that we saw had many more orcs than those we faced in the woods that night. Hundreds of gnolls too. And beasts bigger and more fearsome than those. When we talk of this army outnumbering us, we do not mean one Ranger for every two or three of them, but rather, one Ranger to every ten or fifteen of them. And if one orc is worth five Rangers and they have dozens, maybe hundreds, of these orcs among their ranks, then the odds are even worse. Then there are the beasts that are even larger than the orcs, who are most likely even stronger than the foes we recently fought, making those odds even less in our favor. We saw dark elves riding on top of huge, hairy animals that would dwarf anything in the forest that we are familiar with. There was a caravan of supply carts and siege engines. This was not only a massive army but one that was well supplied and outfitted to wage war on an unprecedented scale."

Still, their words fell on deaf ears as the elders were content in their belief that no such force existed nor that any such force posed a real threat to Rishdel.

"Well," one elder retorted, "the great forest would protect us from any such attack. No force would be able to carry that much equipment through the thick woods in which we dwell. The siege engines would have to be left behind, as would many of their supplies, and their numbers would do little good in the woods that would divide them and give us the advantage."

Another of the elders agreed with his colleague and felt compelled to speak against Riorik and Nordahs as well.

"If such a force exists, which I highly doubt, and they marched with that amount of gear, then it is unlikely that they march on Rishdel."

Elder Bostic listened as the elders voiced their dissenting opinions on the claims. Eventually, after several of the elders had spoken, Elder Bostic had questions of his own.

"So, Riorik," Elder Bostic started as he addressed the young elf, "did you see which way this army marched? Do they march toward Rishdel or somewhere else?"

Nordahs wanted to answer for his friend but knew better. Elder Bostic had asked Riorik directly, so for Nordahs to answer would be disrespectful and would likely incite the elder's wrath. Nordahs had no choice but to let Riorik answer and hope for the best.

"No," Riorik answered. "The army appeared to march East, away from Rishdel. The assumption is the army marches toward the human town on the eastern coast, based on their direction. However—"

But, before he could continue, he was interrupted by Elder Bostic and was forced to quit speaking.

"I see," Elder Bostic said. "Since the army does not march this way, I think there is no immediate danger to Rishdel, and this whole meeting could have waited until a better time."

Elder Bostic's stare focused on Commander Greenblade as he finished his words. Commander Greenblade understood what the elder's statement and glare meant for him. The commander was equal parts embarrassed and angry, but tradition dictated that he not say or do anything until the meeting had adjourned. He had no choice but to remain in his seat and tolerate the judging eyes of the elders that now looked down upon him and blamed him for their unceremonious rousing from sleep.

For Riorik and Nordahs, it was a frustrating end to their mission, but not one that they had not anticipated given their standing in the village, especially Riorik's standing. But as the elders began to rise from their seats in preparation of returning to their slumber, Riorik was struck with an idea.

"Wait!" he exclaimed. "What if our story can be corroborated, and maybe even expanded? Would that not give you a reason for concern?"

Elder Bostic held up his hand and the other elders all stopped. None returned to their seat, but the procession out of the room at least came to a halt.

"And how would you do that?" Elder Bostic asked.

"My brother Kirin," Riorik answered. "He returned here with us tonight and waits at the entrance. He saw this army too, separate from us, and he may have yet more to say about its intentions."

Riorik knew it was a gamble to include Kirin this way, especially since Kirin was unaware of what has and has not been said about his involvement in the ordeal, but Riorik did not think there was any other way to convince the elders of the very real threat that existed. Elder

Bostic hesitated before agreeing to hear what Kirin had to add to the topic before summoning him to the great hall.

The robed elf was escorted into the room and led to the center of the floor to stand in front of the elders, just as Riorik and Nordahs had before.

"Your brother tells us that you have knowledge of a threat against us," Elder Bostic said looking at Kirin.

Kirin quickly looked over at Riorik with great concern and fear. The three had agreed to keep Kirin's true level of involvement a secret, but Elder Bostic's words suggested otherwise. But Riorik gave his brother a subtle shake of his head to let Kirin know that his secret was still safe. The two brothers immediately understood the looks given by the other, so this subtle communication was well understood by each, and Kirin felt a sense of relief from Riorik's response. Now, the wizard just needed to figure out how to answer the elder's question.

"Aye, I do," Kirin slowly replied. "I have seen the same army that Riorik and Nordahs have seen. That is why we all rushed to Rishdel to warn you of it."

"Your brother has told us what he has seen, but we would like to hear what you have to say now," another skeptic elder advised Kirin.

"Well," Kirin started before pausing as he tried to think of what to say, "as part of my training in Mechii, the gnomes sent me off to do some fieldwork where I was to go from town to town offering my services to perform basic magic for people who might need my help. In retrospect, I think it was more of an excuse to get me out of the academy for a while as I had never heard of any other student being sent off like that and most places I went refused my services."

He thought this part would be believable to the elders and give his story a reason for him to be so far away from Mechii.

"After being rejected by many of the towns just north of Mechii, I decided to try my luck in Nectana, just over the border in Narsdin. If I was to find anywhere that might not reject me, I thought it might be there," Kirin said, continuing with this story. "It was in Nectana that I overheard others talking about a fearsome leader in Macadre who wished to wage war against 'those would-be noble races in the south'. The individuals I overheard talking said that he had put together an army of thousands and that they were already marching toward Kern. But it was the next part that really spooked me. Apparently, the two I heard talking were under the belief that this army's leader was in possession of at least one piece of the Ascension Armor."

It was at the mention of the armor that one of the elders interrupted Kirin.

"Aha! Proof that this is just a bunch of poppycock. The armor isn't real, so whatever you thought you heard was likely nothing more than the fantasy of some disgruntled person or someone's wishful thinking."

Kirin took a moment to stare down the elder who interrupted him. Kirin held no regard for the elders, just as they held no regard for him, so tradition and respect for the elders were of little consequence to him.

"May I be allowed to continue? Especially since it was you all who summoned me here to tell this story," Kirin angrily snapped back at the elder.

Everyone else in the room was taken back by Kirin's boldness and was unsure of how to respond. In their stunned silence, Kirin took the opportunity to continue his story.

"Having heard these things, that I too thought were ludicrous, I chose to go on the hunt for this group and this legendary armor wielding leader. The gnomes of Mechii talked of the armor as if it was real but declined to really talk about it with me, so I wanted to know if there was any truth to the stories. I walked out of Nectana and spent the next several days wandering around in the barren wilderness of Narsdin, looking for these troops. Eventually, I did run across them between the sand dunes that cover the area. The number of troops I saw in that formation was staggering. It went beyond the horizon and was more soldiers than I could see or count. I dared not to get close enough to be seen against such overwhelming odds, so I was unable to substantiate the existence of the armor, but given the secrecy in which the gnomes talked about it, I have little doubt that it is real."

"And this army of untold numbers were headed to Kern?" one elder asked.

"Yes, it seemed consistent with the details overheard in Nectana. The astoundingly large group appeared to be heading toward Kern. Everything the two in Nectana said about the force appeared to be true," Kirin answered.

"Everything but the fact that their leader had a piece of the Ascension Armor that is, correct?" another elder asked rather arrogantly.

"I can neither confirm nor deny that claim," Kirin responded. "The gnomes at the mage academy seem convinced that the armor is real, just as the two individuals I overheard in Nectana seemed to think. Everything else about their story was confirmed, so at this point I have no reason to doubt that claim as well. And just because something isn't seen doesn't mean that it is not real or does not exist. Only one's arrogance would lead them to believe that only the things they have seen are real and all others are flights of fancy."

Kirin's repeated jabs at the close-minded elders were beginning to make the whole situation much tenser than it already was.

"That's enough," Riorik softly huffed at his brother, who felt nothing but contempt for the elves that had been the source of his family's shame and suffering in his mind.

There was a tense silence that followed. The elders glared at Kirin, unsure of what to do about his attitude or his story. Kirin stared back at them, waiting to see what else they might say. And Riorik, he stared at Kirin, fearful that his brother would say something else to upset the elders. Riorik desperately wanted to gain their trust and help in confronting Cyrel's army. But, once more, it was Nordahs who spoke up and broke the awkward silence.

"There you have it. The same force observed not once but twice by two different groups. I think we can all agree that the presence of the group is very real, and that while they are not headed to Rishdel now, a force of that size is a very real threat to anyone in their path."

Elder Bostic, the most sensible of the elders, responded in kind to Nordahs' assessment and summary of the situation.

"I would concur that there is little question about if a group of soldiers from Narsdin exist. However, I would disagree that such a force creates a threat for us. Both of you even said that the group marches on Kern. Kern is on the opposite side of our vast landscape, so there is little reason for us to worry. That is a human problem, not ours."

"For elders, you really are a bunch of old fools, aren't you?" Kirin said. "An army of this size does not march on a single town. An army that big means only one thing—conquest. If you do nothing, the other cities will fall, and you will be left to face this threat all alone, and with almost certainly no chance of surviving."

"And what would you have us do, oh great and wise mage?" another elder asked Kirin sarcastically.

"At a minimum, I would post Rangers at the edge of the forest to keep watch for any hostile forces that may move toward Rishdel to give you the most warning possible to prepare your defenses, especially since you think our claims are bogus. Then, I would send messenger birds to all the other cities, warning of a possible invasion from the north so that they may have a chance to defend themselves, since you dare not lift a finger to defend them yourselves. Even if the fight does not come to their doors, they can at least protect themselves just in case. If we truly think ourselves to be better and more 'noble' than those who dwell in the Narsdin region, then we should at least be willing to warn others. If we sit by and do nothing, letting those other cities fall without so much as a word of warning, then we are less noble than the invaders."

"But," he continued, "if you are noble, then you would prepare your troops to aid and defend not just our people but any who may fall in the shadow of this maniacal leader's army and not just wait for them to come knocking on our gates. The Rangers of Rishdel are supposed to defend the land, protect the people, and repel evil. Well, evil is out there, people need protecting, the land needs defending, and right now, you, the leaders of the Rangers of Rishdel, stand there doing nothing."

Riorik could only stare at his brother. Never had he heard Kirin speak with such conviction or pride. Growing up, his older brother tried to keep his head down and voice low to avoid the beatings and mockery that their family's shame seemed to invite at every opportunity. But now, this was a whole new Kirin standing in front of Riorik, and Riorik was filled with great pride to see his brother stand up against the elders and virtually shame them as they had once shamed him.

"Your words are sharp but wise," Elder Bostic eventually conceded. "We are indeed a noble race and have an obligation to help those in need, even if we do not always agree with their ways or opinions. And I see no harm in passing on reports of hostile forces to the other cities. They can decide for themselves what they may want to do about such reports. However, I will not send the forces of this guild away from Rishdel to leave it defenseless unless there is little other choice and our help is requested."

In the end, Elder Bostic dictated a message to be sent to the other cities with instructions to get the birds in the air as quickly as possible. The elders talked with Commander Greenblade to increase the number of scouts and to expand their area to the forest's edge. There was also an edict passed to have the stocks of weapons and supplies checked and corrected as needed, just in case they needed to mobilize every Ranger the guild had to offer. The elders were unwilling to do anything else without more information and eagerly closed the meeting so they could return to their beds.

It was not the answer Riorik had hoped for, but at least the elders agreed to fly the birds to the other cities so that they may be at least warned. Riorik could only hope that the birds reached their destinations before it was too late.

However, this outcome now left Riorik and Nordahs with a new challenge. They had returned to Rishdel and successfully passed off Wuffred's death as a successful end to their mission, but without the Rangers marching off to fight Cyrel Leafwalker and his army, Riorik and Nordahs needed to find a way to leave the village again without getting in trouble. Surely Commander Greenblade would expect them to return to the guild and continue their post among their ranks now.

At this point, Riorik would take what he could get from the elders, and he and Nordahs would just have to figure out another plan to return to their quest, all while keeping the secret of the greaves in Riorik's pack to themselves.

Chapter 9

The massive force left through Kern's southern gate as one giant

conglomerate. Their three destinations were south of the conquered

city, so the plan was to move as one unit, with the different forces

breaking off as each objective was reached. The distance between Kern

and Dresdin, the home of the halflings, was nearly double the distance

between the oasis and Kern, so it would take a while to reach even their first destination, with the cities of Mechii and Rhorm being significantly farther.

The land between Kern and their first destination, Dresdin, was a mix of farmland, the sand dunes extending down from Narsdin at the souther end, rugged mountainous terrain as they neared Barbos, and then lush fields near the halfling village that sat on the other side of the River Via. Unbeknownst to them, the path would also take them right past the site where Baolba and his small expeditionary force had encountered the barbarian huntress Alaricea and the warriors under her command. The orcs and gnolls now marching on the southern cities would pass within close distance to where some of their own relatives had died in combat.

But despite the varying landscapes and the dangerously close passing of the barbarian city, the biggest obstacle that the group faced was the raging river that flowed just north of Dresdin. Dresdin sat nestled near the river's mouth that gulped water in from the sea before washing it downstream and across the entire continent. Such rivers were not to be found in the wastelands of Narsdin. The mountains to the north only harbored small streams filled with the occasional rains or meltwater from the mountain's snowy caps. Few among them had any concept of the challenge that lay ahead.

Undeterred, either by their own ignorance or blind loyalty to their master, the group pressed on through the night toward their targets. By the dawn of morning, the group could easily see mountains to the east. It was the home of the barbarians, but the town of Barbos laid deep in the mountain range on top of a high plateau, far away from the marching mass of soldiers.

What the marching army did not know was that the barbarians were hidden among the mountain's many peaks, caves, and crags, watching as they passed. It should have been of little surprise to anyone that they were being watched as their movements were anything but quiet. Hundreds and thousands of footsteps thundering as they marched in unison. The sound echoed through the mountains, so even if the barbarians had not already been on high alert, they would have certainly be alerted to such a massive force's presence then.

The barbarian forces, recognizing just how overwhelmingly outnumbered they were, chose not to reveal their presence to the passing force. Instead, the powerful fighters watched as the full group moved past the mountains. Villkir[4], leader of the barbarian observers, waited until he was certain the massive force was not headed toward Barbos and headed out of sight before he signaled his men to rally on his position.

"It seems that our fears were right," Villkir started. "The foul beasts that came before have come again, only this time we will be ready."

He turned to two older, obviously experienced barbarian fighters, "Bror[5], Dhun[6], I need the two of you to follow that behemoth of an army and send reports back on where they are headed. I will have others posted along behind you as runners to ferry information back and forth."

"Understood, Villkir," Bror, the older of the two barbarians, said as he acknowledged the command.

"What will you do, Villkir?" asked Dhun.

There was no tone of anger or jealousy in Dhun's voice but rather just one of curiosity. What they had all just witnessed was

---

[4] Pronounced "V-ill-cur"
[5] Pronounced "B-roar"
[6] Pronounced "Dune"

someone terrifying, and Dhun wanted to know what Villkir's thoughts were and nothing more.

"I will return to Barbos and let the others know that the beasts are back and in greater numbers. It is not for me to decide the fate of our people on my own. I must take it to the council and let them vote on if we act, do nothing, or make for the boats to finally leave this land. Whatever their decision, I will be sure to forward it on to you immediately, this I promise you."

"I know you will, brother," Dhun responded before exchanging a hearty handshake with Villkir.

"Let's go and see where these foul things are headed," Dhun said to Bror before the pair sped off down the mountain paths toward where the other group had only recently passed by.

Villkir then turned to the others there also under his command.

"Divide yourselves up in pairs. Space each pairing out evenly between Barbos and those two. Try to keep the distances fair and even as you will be relaying information back and forth as they observe whatever that was that we just watched go by and whatever decisions the council provides in relation to that. If the gap begins to get too far apart and you do not think it safe to continue, let me know, and I will decide what to do next. But, for now, I must be off to let the council

know what we just saw."

There was a collective salute from the group to Villkir and his

orders. The dozen remaining barbarians wasted no time in pairing up

into the groups just as Villkir had said and set about trying to gauge

distances as they moved into the relay positions demanded by their

leader. Meanwhile, Villkir did not wait around to see his words put into

action. He simply returned the salute and walked off.

***

Villkir effortlessly pushed his way through the gate that separated

Barbos from the outside world. He walked along the main street of

town toward a large, oval-shaped building and its thatch roof. White,

wispy smoke curled out of an opening near the building's center. Villkir

knew the smoke meant that at least some of the council was in the

building, which was most of the time.

The council oversaw the entire village and their overseas affairs.

No building was built, no ship was launched, and no trade commerce

was conducted without the council's knowledge and approval. The

same was for war. Since the days of old, the council, elected by the residents of Barbos every five years, determined everything that was to be done or not done for every barbarian that lived there. It was a dramatic departure from how the other races and cities operated. Where others were largely based on a feudal system, Barbos operated more like a democracy than anything else.

"You all were right to be concerned," Villkir blurted out as he strode right through the doors and into the council's building.

There were no rooms in the oblong building. It was only a single open space with a long table that sat in its center. Around the table sat the council members, numbered twenty-four in total. But on this day, only a handful were at the table when Villkir made his entrance. Even still, those in the room immediately gave their attention to the unexpected intrusion.

"The beasts responsible for Alaricea's death have returned," Villkir continued, now that he had their attention. "However, they moved south, past Barbos."

"Did you confront them?" asked one of the robust barbarians sitting around the table.

"No," Villkir answered. "Their numbers are great. Much greater than ours were then, and even much more than ours could be now. If they had turned this way, I think we would have little chance at repelling their advances. It is a much larger force now than what we suspect Alaricea fought against. It is likely that she only encountered an advance guard, and this is their main force."

"And they passed our village by?" asked another of the council members.

"Yes, they continued south, past the mountain trails that would lead them here," Villkir answered.

"Then perhaps they are too afraid of a real fight and opted to not anger the mighty barbarians of Barbos," bellowed the fat barbarian, who had apparently spent more time eating and drinking around the council table than anything else.

"Whatever their reasons are for passing us by, we cannot deny that they are here, and Alaricea still needs to be avenged," countered Villkir, who felt disdain for the fat council member who he felt was a poor excuse for a 'real' barbarian.

"I know you want revenge for your wife's death," responded the fat barbarian, "but if this force is as big as you say, we cannot simply go chasing after them and expect a different outcome than before."

As much as Villkir despised him, Villkir could not deny the words he spoke. If Villkir rushed to confront the enormous group that he had just seen, then he would certainly die just like his wife had, and he knew it.

"Didn't Alaricea's brother, Whilem, say something in a message recently about 'a dark cloud of reckoning' forming in Macadre and that he planned to intervene after we sent word of his sister's death?" the first council member asked aloud to the group.

"He did, but we have not heard a word from him since," answered the fat council member.

"He said something about working with a group of rogues or something near Tyleco who he would get information from at times," said another council member. "Perhaps if we send word to Tyleco, we can glean more insight and maybe even learn Whilem's current whereabouts."

"Our so-called 'cousins' are not likely to give us much," replied an old barbarian that hobbled through the door behind Villkir with the help of a cane.

"Our human relatives have had little to do with us in many years. Even our traders are poorly welcomed in their towns. Why else do you think we have turned to the seas for commerce? Regardless, it might be worth sending a bird there to see if we can hear word from Whilem. Our last couple of birds sent to Nectana have gone unanswered, so it is not as if we have much to lose by trying."

The other council members apparently had much respect for the old codger as there was no discussion or dissent given to his opinion. Instead, the immediate topic became what should be sent to Tyleco and how quickly could they make that happen.

"Villkir, I know this is asking a lot as you have waited for their return to get your revenge," the old barbarian said as he stood next to Villkir with his hand on his shoulder. "But let us wait to see what response we get from Tyleco and, hopefully, Whilem. A force as big as you described will require the help of others if we wish to avoid a similar fate."

The wise old barbarian's words humbled Villkir. He had yearned for a chance to kill those who had taken his beloved wife from him, and now he was being asked to wait even longer. But not without good reason.

Villkir proceeded to tell the council the orders he had issued to those under his command and how the runners would relay information to and fro. The council was quick to congratulate Villkir on his quick thinking and that their continued observation of this unknown group would prove valuable in the coming days.

As Villkir exited the building, not happy but content with the council's approach, he sent word to Bror and Dhun that their orders remained the same and now had the council's blessing. All that Villkir could do now was wait for news from his scouts and any response from the bird flying toward Tyleco.

***

Ammudien and Rory wasted no time in putting some distance between them and Tyleco after their ground-smashing and glass-shattering escape from Lord Veyron's throne room. They were certain that Lord Veyron would send his troops after them, especially if he thought the pair still carried his precious shield with them, which they did. To Ammudien, this was just as good as if Lord Veyron had offered to send help to Kern.

"Come on, we need to leave before the guards find us," Rory said as he tugged on Ammudien's sleeve.

"No, wait," Ammudien said. "You're headed in the wrong direction."

"What do you mean? The only wrong direction here is back toward Tyleco. I'm headed to Brennan."

"Yeah, but do you not see? This is perfect for our cause," countered Ammudien.

"How so?" a confused Rory asked.

"We wanted Lord Veyron to send his troops to aid Kern, right? Well, now his troops are on the move. We only need to lead them to where we want. He lusts for this shield even more now than he did before, so he will not stop until he has it. We can go toward Kern and his troops will have no choice but to follow, and then he will see for himself that what we said was true."

"And what makes you so certain that he will see any of this?" Rory questioned.

"Easy," started Ammudien. "Now that he knows this is the Shield of Sagrim, he will not allow any of his soldiers to possess it, and he will want to take it for himself as soon as he can because he sees this as his path to the throne of thrones among you humans. He will not risk anyone else using it to usurp his power."

"Then, let's head to Kern," Rory gladly agreed.

"Not so fast," Ammudien cautioned. "We know that Cyrel's army was headed to Kern, but we do not know where around Kern they may be. And there is a good chance that Lord Veyron's goons are already out searching for us. I need to find us a safe path first."

"Whatever you're going to do, do it quick," urged Rory.

Ammudien wasted no time in taking up position in a flat area nearby.

"Do not move," he told Rory as he started casting his detection spell.

Rory watched in amazement at the whole spectacle. He had seen Ammudien cast this spell before, but the whole idea of magic was still new and awe-inspiring to him. The gnome's hands glowed once again while Rory watched as Ammudien's head tilted from side to side and turned down toward the ground, like he was trying to listen or focus. The whole event only lasted a minute or two before Ammudien shook the glow from his hands and walked back to Rory's location.

"I fear we may be too late to help Kern," Ammudien said solemnly. "I felt the movement of a lot of feet, too many feet to be a herd of animals—only an army. They were south of Kern and moving toward Mechii. I fear my hometown may be next, but now I am without a way to get word to them to warn of the coming danger."

"Maybe Kern repelled them," Rory suggested. "Maybe they move south looking for an easier target."

"An easier target they will not find at Mechii. The magic barriers around our city have held for centuries and are said to be impenetrable," Ammudien said aloud, more to reassure himself than to counter Rory's suggestion.

"And," the mage continued, "I do not think that Kern repelled them. I did not feel the presence of any force following them, and they did not move with a sense of urgency. No, I think Kern fell and fell quickly, and now they are on to their next target."

"So, what do we do?" the concerned guard captain pondered aloud.

"I suggest we continue with our plan— head toward Kern, and hopefully lead Lord Veyron's troops there. If they see Kern in ruins or can liberate its people from any force that remains, then maybe we can convince Lord Veyron to stand against Cyrel's dark intentions and maybe even help garner support from the other human towns. He needs to see that we did not lie about that threat."

"And did you detect any movement consistent with Lord Veyron looking for us?" Rory asked, just wanting to confirm if Ammudien's plan was worth the risk.

"Most definitely," Ammudien answered. "I could sense several horses being saddled and brought out for riders and the fast, running footsteps where the guardhouse barracks were located. There is no doubt in my mind that he is sending the full force of Tyleco after us."

Having heard that, Rory quickly agreed with Ammudien's plan, and the pair set a course for Kern. It was not without risk though as their path would take them across the path of the Tyleco forces hunting them. It was the only way to guarantee that Lord Veyron and his troops would follow them. The big fear was Tyleco's mounted forces. They would be able to move faster than Ammudien and Rory could on foot.

But the crafty gnome quickly devised a plan to counter that advantage. Ammudien and Rory would make themselves and their path known to the men following them. Then, once the troops were following them but before the horsemen could catch them, Ammudien would use his magic to make the pair of them invisible. That way they did not have to worry about the troops seeing them, the horses catching them, or the archers taking aim on them. Their only worry would be if their tracks in the dirt and sand between Tyleco and Kern would give them away.

Either way, it was a risk they were willing to take if it achieved their goal.

***

"Hurry up and get some men on those horses!" yelled Lord Veyron. "And where is my horse?"

"Your horse is coming, Lord Veyron," one of his valets told him. "It has been some time since you rode out like this, so your saddle required cleaning before being affixed to your steed. But rest assured that your glorious mount will be here at any moment."

The valet was very nervous about telling Lord Veyron of the delay. It was the responsibility of the stablemaster to keep all of the gear in tip-top shape and ready for riding at a moment's notice. For the attendant to tell Lord Veyron that his saddle required cleaning before use was an indictment against the stablemaster and his failure to perform his duties. Depending on Lord Veyron's mood, such a failure could be met with a simple reprimand or death, but considering Lord Veyron's current mood, it did not look good for the stablemaster's future.

"What about the men on the wall? Have they not found them yet?" Lord Veyron yelled in frustration.

"They are still looking, my lord," one of the men on the wall replied. "We think we have seen where the rock crashed just beyond the wall, but we did not spy the fugitives in the area. They must already have fled."

"Of course they have fled!" shouted Lord Veyron in response to the guard's assessment of the obvious.

"We must find them and catch them," Lord Veyron continued. "Rory Cooper has turned his back on his oath and his city. He has deserted his post to join forces with that dastardly gnome who has stolen MY shield!"

During Lord Veyron's tirade, the stablemaster finally emerged from the stables with Lord Veyron's freshly polished leather saddle. It was quickly placed on his horse's well-groomed, white-haired back. The silver buckles were fastened to hold the sturdy saddle in place. The black and tan leather bridle and reigns, adorned with silver studs and decorations, stood out against the elegant horse's white hair and long, yellow mane. There was only one horse in all of Tyleco with such a distinct and stunning look, so it only stood to reason that such a magnificent beast would be in Lord Veyron's royal stable as his personal mount.

With his horse's tack finally in place and ready to ride, Lord Veyron wasted no time in stepping into the finely crafted silver stirrups that hung from his saddle to take a seat in his magnificent saddle. He quickly grabbed the reigns and immediately started tugging on them, prompting his horse to start moving.

"We ride now!" he demanded as he angled his horse toward the nearest gate out of town. "Anyone who is not ready faces fifty lashes."

The last sentiment sparked a flurry of furious activity as the men not on horses hustled to get on one. Nobody wanted to receive lashes as a form of punishment. Lord Veyron, who was not known for dishing out corporal punishments often, took great pride though in having hired one of the meanest, cruelest torturers and executioner in all Corsallis. Usually, just the thought of getting lashes by the angry, hulking man in Lord Veyron's employment was enough to scare most people straight. For Lord Veyron to so openly and willingly decree that his men would receive lashes for not being on their horses quicker was an obvious sign to how angry and how serious their lord was about the current situation.

It did not take long for the entire mounted garrison to be ready. The group of horses and men rode out of town to the thundering sound of hooves clattering on the city's cobblestone streets. Some of the men wore lightweight leather armor and made little other noise, but some of the ones near the group's rear wore chainmail coifs or shirts that could be heard clinking as the metal links rattled together under the horse's movements.

"Bring the rest to our position as quickly as you can," Lord Veyron shouted to Captain Feigh, who was helping man the city's gate as the horses and their riders galloped past and out into the lands beyond the city's walls.

"And see that my stablemaster finds a new home in the dungeon," Captain Feigh heard his lord and master call out as the group moved off into the distance. He was not sure the reason for his lord's command, but the reason was inconsequential, it was an order and was

expected to be followed. Otherwise, it could be Captain Feigh who

found himself in the dungeon, and he knew it.

Chapter 10

The first bird from Rishdel arrived in Brennan. It was the closest town to the elven village. The message was quickly forwarded to Draynard, the Bandit King of Brennan, who had ambushed Skeel and his party of orcs and gnolls just outside the city weeks earlier. Draynard read the message, and his thoughts immediately returned to the much smaller force that he and his men had executed before.

"A massive force from the North," he thought to himself as he contemplated the message's meaning.

Draynard was instantly reminded of the Skeel's offer of wealth if the bandits helped them find a treasure for their master. The Bandit King began to think there was more truth to the gnoll's story than he had first thought. But either way, it was too late, he had already killed the gnoll, so there was no chance to get any more information from the dog-like beast.

But the bigger question on the Bandit King's mind was why he had not heard of this force sooner. The message from the elves talked about the force marching toward Kern, but he had not received any word from his spies there that might confirm the message. Part of Draynard's mind felt that this was some new elven trick or a ruse from some other town that hoped to draw his bandit forces out of Brennan for their own nefarious purposes. Surely, if there was an army of this size near Kern, he would have heard about it from his spies there, he thought to himself. And the silence from Kern seemed to say more to the Bandit King than the note he currently held in his hand.

That feeling of suspicion was shortlived though. Only moments after the bird from Rishdel arrived, another bird, this one from Tyleco, arrived. It seemed as if one of his spies there had sent urgent word to Draynard too.

'Draynard,

Veyron's token has gone missing. Stolen by a gnome and one of Veyron's own guards before fleeing Tyleco. Veyron rides after them with his other troops following behind. Only a few guards will remain in the city. If you were to ever take Tyleco for your own, now is the time. They ride East, toward Kern, in pursuit of the thieves. Avoid that area at all costs for the time being.

Also, we heard talk that an unknown force was operating near Kern. Is there competition now? Is someone else moving into our territory? Have the barbarians given up on trade and decided to try and beat us at our own game?

Signed,

X'

This second message talking about an unknown force and Kern was enough to give Draynard reason to pause and have a concern. It was apparent that his agent in Tyleco knew that something was going on that drew Lord Veyron's troops toward Kern. He wondered if the gnome thief mentioned in the message was a part of that unknown force and if Veyron was headed to fight, or if it was merely a coincidence that the two messages arrived at the same time and talked of similar events near the town of Kern.

In Draynard's experience, coincidence were not real. All things happened for a reason and usually through the calculated thoughts of someone. The Bandit King began to work through his thoughts.

"If this was a ruse by someone to draw me away from Brennan, it must be a coordinated effort from many towns to have messages sent from Rishdel and Tyleco," he thought first.

"But there have been no missives about an elf in Tyleco recently. Nor have there been any reports of an emissary from Tyleco heading off to Rishdel. So, either the two groups would have had to meet in a neutral location or use a go-between to form this alliance. It would be unlikely for them to operate with this precision of sending two birds almost simultaneously without significant planning and communication, which I would have surely heard about."

Then, the Bandit King remembered another critical piece of information.

Several of the bandits that had been camped outside of Tyleco had failed to send reports and payments from recent activities. After a few days, Draynard had sent word to one of his spies in Tyleco to check on them, and the report returned seemed to echo his own experience but with the opposite outcome. His agent described what looked like a fight scene between gnolls and orcs, just like he had outside of Brennan, but that this time the bandits had lost. He had forgotten the details of the fight because, at the time, he was most upset by the news that no loot was found at the site.

Now, Draynard had information about two groups of orcs and gnolls clashing with him and his bandits. This gave validity to the warning from the elves. Then, both the report from Rishdel and the report from Tyleco mention Kern. The Bandit King refused to dismiss that simply as coincidence. But, he decided he needed more information before acting on such vague and risky information.

"Send a bird to our man in Kern asking for a status report," Draynard ordered one of his men, who promptly set off to see his order fulfilled.

"Also," he said, talking to another bandit nearby, "send a scout to Kern just in case."

He walked around the dark, dank basement where he liked to conduct business. He was the undisputed leader of Brennan who, as part of a bastard lineage of the last human king, had his own claims to the human thrones. But he had long preferred to operate in the shadows, so even now he did not rule from a throne but from the underground. As Brennan was mostly made up of scoundrels, rogues, and thieves, nobody minded Draynard's subterranean tendencies.

"Gather the other men," he said as his final order.

"Tyleco may finally be ripe for a raid if one report is true. But, if another report is accurate, we may very well need to be ready to fight for our very survival," Draynard added as his final order was set into motion.

***

One of the bird keeper's errand boys came sprinting up to Captain Feigh. The young boy gasped for air, unable to find the breath to utter a word as he held up the rolled message parchment. Feigh just stared at the boy as he was doubled over, desperate for air but unable to find enough. The boy started shaking his held up fist with the note in it at the surprised captain.

"An urgent message for Lord Veyron," the boy eventually gasped.

Captain Feigh swiped the note from the messenger's hand and quickly unrolled it. As the newly appointed captain of the guard, he was the highest-ranking person in the city, with Lord Veyron and the others out pursuing Ammudien and Rory. This meant that such messages were forwarded to him, and it was his responsibility to act on them or forward them on to someone else.

Reading the unfurled note, he quickly recognized it as coming from Rishdel. Despite the message being written in the common tongue of the humans, the elves' unmistakable flourish was obvious in the elegant calligraphy.

But it was what the message said that caught Captain Feigh's attention more than the handwriting. Just as the message to Brennan had warned, this note spoke of a large army marching south toward Kern. This was of great concern to Feigh, considering that was the direction Lord Veyron and his men had just ridden off toward. And what was worse, many of the other men under his command had followed behind. There were few others in Tyleco left to send after Lord Veyron to warn him of another threat. But the worst thing was that Lord Veyron had taken every horse with him in pursuit of the so-called 'thieves', so even if there was someone he could spare to take this message to Lord Veyron, he had no way to expedite its delivery.

It was quite a quandary for the recently promoted guard captain. Since he was the highest-ranking person left in Tyleco, he was responsible for the city's protection and could not leave to deliver the message himself. He had only a dozen or so men left under his control, so he could not spare a single soldier to take the message to Lord Veyron. And, if he found someone to take the message, there were no horses left in Tyleco that someone could use to catch up to Lord Veyron's fast-moving group.

In the end, all Captain Feigh could do was nothing. At least Lord Veyron traveled with the might of Tyleco, so even if they did encounter this mystery group in the elven warning, then he would have ample protection. Or, at least, that is what he told himself as he tried to rationalize his lack of action in his own mind.

"Have there been any other messages recently?" Feigh asked the boy, who had finally caught his breath.

"Only one," the boy answered. "It came from Barbos and was addressed to a Whilem, but we've had no luck finding anyone with that name.

"Return the message saying as much," Captain Feigh commanded.

"But," he quickly added as he thought about it, "add a note that we have heard rumors of a hostile force near Barbos and Kern. Then, ask if they have seen or heard anything. And do not dawdle, this needs to be sent immediately."

Feigh thought it was a long shot but figured it worth asking. If anything, he might be able to dispel any thoughts or concerns about Lord Veyron's safety if the barbarians refuted the elves' claim.

The errand boy turned, and even though he did not really want to, sprinted back toward the bird keeper's home to send Captain Feigh's message to Barbos, just as the captain had wanted.

***

The small hamlet of Dresdin began to draw within view of the marching army just as day began to break the following morning. It was a very small settlement. Dresdin was the home of the halflings, pretty much anybody who claimed to be of half-gnome or half-dwarf heritage, but mostly half dwarf. Back before the great segregation of races, there were a lot of elves and humans that got involved with dwarves. It was less about romance and more about greed, though, in many of those relationships since the dwarves controlled the gold, silver, and gemstone mines. Others always wanted to align themselves with the dwarves for the money and power they thought the connections would bring.

But, after the races of Corsallis closed their gates to one another, there was suddenly no home for those born from those ill-gotten relationships. The elven and human parents, who had gotten little in terms of money or power following the racial divide, turned away their half-breed children in hopes of starting anew with someone of their own race, while those same children were shunned and pushed out by their dwarven or gnomish parents under the threat by others of having their family's property taken away if they did not.

It was indeed a sad time in Corsallis to have families torn apart by such racial ways of thinking, but it was 'abide by society's rule or find a new home'. Many opted to join the collective society's way of thinking, regardless of whether it was right or not, because it was the path of least resistance and it allowed them to keep the cozy lifestyles they had become accustomed to having.

The southern region of Turkin[7] found itself full of homeless half-dwarf or half-gnome residents. Eventually, through a shared experience, the group of half breeds banded together and chose to start their own town. Dresdin started as a small shanty town full of destitute individuals and a few families, but over the years, individuals came together to start their own families, and the families put their skills to work to form businesses and farms that produced goods for everyone else in their quaint little village. It became their own socialist environment, in which everyone had a stake in every aspect of the town. Any food produced was produced for everyone, and those skilled in textiles and weaving produced goods to be used by everyone else.

This dependency on one another kept strife and violence among the town's residents to a minimum, but,at the same time, the lack of a need or desire for money meant that everyone in town was considered poor outside of their village. There was nothing to be gained by bandits trying to rob the village, and Dresdin occupied land that was of little strategic value or harbored resources that could be used for

---

[7] Pronounced "Tur-kin"

manufacturing, so there was little threat from other nearby towns. As such, Dresdin had no defensive structures or even a trained army. Despite their small statures, the people of Dresdin felt completely safe within their homes and town as they worked day by day to eke out an existence.

Little did the town's residents know of the horrors that were headed their way, as a small detachment of gnolls and a single troll broke free from the main pack and turned toward Dresdin.

In the early morning's light, the farmers exited their sod homes with their grass-covered roofs, headed to work in the fields. Their work was quickly interrupted by the arrival of the sprinting gnolls. The first of the unsuspecting farmers were quickly taken down by the blitzing attacks. With no armor or weapons, the gnolls were able to easily use their claws to kill and maim anyone they could get close to.

Most of the gnolls were able to kill two or three farmers each before the others could scramble back inside their homes. One family was not very lucky when they failed to get their door closed in time, and a gnoll slipped inside. Confined in their home with nowhere to hide and little to defend themselves with, the family was easy pickings for the gnoll's savage brutality.

Their screams echoed out from the simple dirt home. For anyone who was not already aware of the death that had arrived, the screams of those dying violent deaths in that home served as a wakeup call and a notice that things in the town of Dresdin were far from peaceful.

Gnolls pummeled doors, scratched through the mud brick walls, and jumped at windows, desperate to get inside to their terrified prey. The people of Dresdin not only represented the targets of their master's bloodlust but also an easy meal of fresh meat, something the gnolls had not feasted on since beginning the long march from the oasis days earlier. But, try as they might, the gnolls found the simple homes to be more resilient than expected.

In the end, it was the group's lone troll that proved to be their salvation. The troll stood several feet above the gnolls. It would have towered over even the orcs that traveled with the main group. It had long, skinny, pointed ears on the side of its hairless head. Its square-shaped head was punctuated with two small tusks that jutted out from the troll's chin. The troll wore only a pair of ragged cloth pants to cover its groin while its chest remained bare. Its brown, leathery skin bore the scars of someone who was familiar with violence.

The powerful troll lumbered into town well after the much quicker gnolls but immediately noticed the gnolls' struggles to get at the residents already barricaded inside their homes. The massive monster walked to the nearest hut where a gnoll was failing to get inside. With a quick brush of his hand, the troll knocked the gnoll away from the house with a yelp. Next, the troll shoved his enormous hands through the open window and grabbed both sides of the wall that held the opening in place. Then, with what looked like an effortless tug, the troll pulled the entire side of the abode apart, leaving a gaping hole for the waiting gnoll to enter through.

The troll stood by the opening to prevent anyone from escaping while the gnoll chased the home's occupants around what remained of their home, killing them one by one. The dirt floor was soaked with blood as more and more screams rang out.

Seeing the ease in which the troll gained entrance to the home, the other gnolls quickly stopped exhausting themselves to wait for their turn. The troll moves from house to house, breaking through what little security was offered. In some cases, the troll would kick the door open, often sending it flying from its attachments. Other times, it would smash its forearm through walls. And even in one case, the giant creature slammed both hands on the roof of a house, sending the entire roof collapsing in on the terrified people inside and trapping them under the debris, making them easy pickings for the slobbering, hungry gnoll waiting outside.

The whole attack on Dresdin lasted only minutes, but in that short, terrible time, everyone in Dresdin had been wiped out. The halfling race had been removed in its entirety by this menacing, genocidal force. A group of people who had existed in peace for generations was now gone.

With their job done, the gnolls and lone troll fled the ruins. There was still a good chance that they could catch up to the others in time to join the raid on Mechii.

***

"Oh, my word," gasped Dhun as he watched the horrors in Dresdin unfold from his vantage point.

He and Bror had followed the group, but when the two barbarians saw the small group split apart, Dhun decided to follow them. The barbarian scout did not know what to expect from such a small group, but the extreme savagery and total annihilation of Dresdin was the last thing that crossed his mind.

Dhun wanted to aid the helpless halflings, but he knew that he was no match for the troll. He thought that he might be able to take the gnolls on his own, which was a gross overestimation of his own skills, but at least he knew better than to think that he could overpower a troll that would look down on him as he would look down on a dwarf.

There was nothing he could do but watch and then return to Bror, so they could report the atrocity to Villkir.

Once he was certain that the assault on Dresdin had ended and his position was still safe, Dhun wasted no time in returning to Bror's position behind the group's main force.

"They just completely wiped out Dresdin," he told Bror somberly.

"What do you mean 'wiped out'?" Bror asked, trying to get clarity from his companion.

"I mean that they went in there and murdered every last individual in Dresdin. It is no longer a town but a graveyard," Dhun answered to Bror's absolute dismay.

"What was there to gain by that?" Bror wondered aloud as he struggled to understand why someone would decimate the defenseless, non-threatening halflings.

"I do not know, but one thing is certain, there was no hesitation or remorse in their actions. We will all be victims of their unbridled brutality if we do nothing," Dhun answered.

"What can we do? We can't exactly take on an army of that size, just the two of us," Bror countered.

"Not just us two but everyone in Corsallis," Dhun clarified.

"I don't know why they are here or what they want. But I can tell you that based on what I just saw, this is a fight for survival, and nobody else yet knows it. We need to get word to Villkir and have them try to warn everybody they can. It might be too late for the people of Dresdin, but maybe there's still time to save others," Dhun added.

"I will go to the nearest runner and get word to Villkir," Bror replied. "You have done enough, now it's my turn," he said to his friend, who was still visibly shaken and disturbed by the villainy and total disregard for life that he had just witnessed.

"No," Dhun said, grabbing Bror's arm before he could leave. "I saw it, I should report it. This is my duty."

Bror could see the anger mixed with supreme sadness in Dhun's eyes and knew that this was something his friend not only felt obligated to do as part of their mission but also responsible for out of respect for the dozens of lives he watched taken in Dresdin.

"Speed be with you, my friend," Bror offered, giving in to Dhun's request and letting him be the one to deliver the message to the nearest runner a few miles behind the pair.

Dhun stood up, wiped the welling tears from his eyes, and broke out in a dead sprint as fast as he could manage toward the runner's expected position.

***

Toby, exhausted from his run out of the tunnels under Kern to Barbos and its mountainous elevation, passed out as he tried to speak to the guards standing watch along the trail leading to the barbarian city. Unsure of who this strange human was or what compelled him to run as he had, the barbarian tossed the limp human over his shoulder and carried him into the city.

"This human came running up the trail and just collapsed at my feet without saying a word," the guard told the barbarian medic he had taken the unconscious Toby to.

"Well, I guess sit him down over there," the medic said as he pointed to a nearby bed, "and I'll take a look at him. You don't suppose he's dangerous, do you?"

"We didn't find any weapons on him, and he was not running at us like he meant us harm. No, it was more of an expression of relief when he saw us. I have no reason to think that he's dangerous," the barbarian guard replied.

"Still, probably best that we restrain the stranger, especially in light of recent events," the medic said while using thin leather strips to tie Toby's arms and legs to the bed's sides.

"There, that should do it," the old medic said as he tied the final strap into place.

"That'd never hold a barbarian," sniffed the guard at the medic's choice of restraints.

"Then I guess it's a good thing that he's not a barbarian," the medic shot back, clearly annoyed by the guard second-guessing his decision.

"Now what?" the guard asked, still puzzled by Toby's sudden and unexpected appearance.

"He looks dehydrated and exhausted. There isn't much else we can do but wait until he is rested and comes back around to find out more," the medic answered.

"You can't smack him around or anything to wake him up sooner?" the guard asked.

Curiosity was beginning to get the better of him.

"I could, but I won't. How would you like it if I woke you up like that?" huffed the stooped over medic sarcastically.

"Now," the medic continued as he poked the guard in the chest with his finger, pushing the guard back toward the door to his home, "you need to return to your post immediately. If the stranger wakes up and has anything to say, then I will take responsibility for alerting those of interest."

The guard knew the medic was right. There was nothing else for him to do there, and it was best for him to return to his post. He did not argue with the old healer but instead turned and left the house to return to his assigned duties along the mountain trail.

***

"Sir, a bird from Rishdel," announced a guard as he held the bird with the note still neatly attached to its foot.

The man slid the note out of the thin tube before unrolling the parchment.

"Hmm, a little late now," he said as he read the message.

"What does it say?" questioned the guard.

The bird keeper turned to the guard with a frown on his face.

"It's a warning about an invading force headed here," Kern's bird keeper said as he stood in the field of arrow-filled birds.

"It's one thing to invade us, it's another to kill all of my birds," he said as he continued slowly walking around and picking up the dead birds.

To him, there was no more gruesome a scene than the sight of his beloved birds' massacre. He cared more for those birds than he did any person. He wept while picking them up and placing them each into their own box. He planned to bury his feathered friends. He would often reminisce aloud to himself about memories he had of each bird all the while. It was a sad scene indeed.

"Who should we deliver the message to?" asked the guard, who was still standing there watching the bird keeper continue his efforts as if the guard was not there.

"There is no one to deliver such a message to," huffed the bird keeper.

"You all have pledged your fealty to our new overlord, and the invasion is complete. This is no longer a warning but a footnote in history," he added before wading the parchment up in his hands and tossing it to the ground.

The young guard was unsure of what to do next, so he remained there, watching the sad bird keeper collect his fallen comrades.

"Either lend a hand to what I'm doing or go back to where you came from," the bird keeper eventually told the guard. "There's nothing left to do here, so help or leave."

The guard, overwhelmed by the sadness in the bird keeper's voice, opted to lend a hand in helping the man respectfully collect and honor his birds.

Chapter 11

"Commander Greenblade, sir?" Riorik said gently as he tried to get his

commander's attention as he strolled past in the hallway.

"What is it, Ranger?" he casually responded as he would to

anyone else in the guild.

Commander Greenblade was of mixed emotions to have Cyrel's

son back in the guild. On one hand, Riorik had seemingly completed

his objective in killing the berserker, which was no small feat in the

commander's mind and a testament to Riorik's desire to please the guild since he willingly agreed to kill his friend. But on the other hand, Commander Greenblade was still distrustful of the son of a traitor and annoyed that the elders had given Riorik an entrance into the guild to begin with. But despite his feelings on the subject, Commander Greenblade was a Ranger and he vowed to treat all other Rangers equally, even Riorik and even though it pained him to do so.

"Nordahs and I were talking about what we saw," Riorik said, immediately jumping to his point. "We, with your permission, of course, would like to leave on a scouting mission to find that army's current position and track them. You know, just in case they start to turn toward Rishdel or their activities give away their ultimate goal, we can rush back and let you and the elders know."

The reality of the situation was that Riorik and Nordahs just wanted to rejoin their friends and use their new knowledge about the armor to stop Cyrel's forces. He could not say that to Commander Greenblade, who had no idea that Riorik's pack held a piece of the armor as they spoke, but the young elf thought this ruse might work.

He was wrong.

"Elder Bostic has already ordered a unit to do just that," Commander Greenblade replied.

"What?" Riorik blurted out before thinking about who he was speaking to.

"Excuse me, Ranger?" the commander questioned with obvious annoyance at the lack of respect Riorik had given his rank.

"Oh, I, um, ah," Riorik stuttered and stammered as he quickly realized his mistake.

The last several weeks that he had spent running around with his friends had made Riorik forget about the pomp and circumstance that comes with addressing people in a military setting like this. Those of higher rank were accustomed to a certain level of respect and constraint from those ranked below them, and Commander Greenblade was certainly no exception.

"I'm sorry, sir," Riorik finally said, once he had a moment to remember his place within the guild. "What I mean to say is, I would like to request that Nordahs and I join that effort. We have familiarity with the area and force in question. I feel our experience with this matter would be invaluable."

Commander Greenblade stared at Riorik, utterly expressionless. Riorik could not determine if his commander agreed with that assessment or if he thought it was the most ludacris thing ever said.

"I'm sure you do," the commander finally said back to Riorik, "but those are not the orders you are to receive."

These words were a blow to Riorik's plan. It sent a gut-wrenching pain through his body as he thought about Ammudien and Rory having to carry on alone. This was the risk of them returning, they all knew that, but Riorik had refused to be deterred by any risks.

"You and Nordahs are to head to Kern," Commander Greenblade continued.

It took a moment for Riorik to realize what the commander was telling him. The young elf was so focused on being separated from his other friends in a time of such danger that he almost ignored Commander Greenblade's words. Of course, once he heard them, Riorik could not help but grin from pointy ear to pointy ear.

"If the information provided is correct," Commander Greenblade continued, "then by the time you arrive in Kern, any assault on the city will likely be complete. We need to study the aftermath to understand their tactics and weapons. Did they charge the gates with their forces? Did they pummel the town with a barrage of projectiles from siege weapons? Did they burn the town to the ground? Did they kill the residents, take them hostage, or conscript them into the army? These are the things we need to know so that we may be as prepared as possible should it come to the Rangers of Rishdel being deployed against this unknown foe."

"Yes, sir!" Riorik exclaimed as he eagerly accepted his new mission without question. "Are we to leave immediately?"

"Yes, you and Nordahs are to leave as soon as you both can be ready," Riorik's commander answered.

"Should I inform Nordahs of the new mission or is that something you can handle, Ranger?" Commander Greenblade asked the giddy Riorik.

"I will pass on your orders, sir," Riorik quickly responded before turning and quickly walking away from the commander and toward his friend.

Riorik could barely concentrate he was so happy to not only find a way out of Rishdel and back to the fight but also with the guild's permission to leave. It was certainly the last thing he expected, given their long absence from the guild, not to mention that Wuffred's death was not something they were responsible for.

***

"Send word to Mechii and Rhorm immediately! They must know of the threat that heads their way," Villkir demanded of the council after hearing Dhun's report about what he witnessed at Dresdin.

"What business is it of ours to get involved?" questioned one of the many council members now seated around the long table in the middle of the room.

Villkir was flabbergasted at the council member's lack of compassion and empathy for the people of Dresdin. He struggled to find the words to respond to such a heartless question.

"Because," Villkir finally began, "they came to our home and killed my wife. We did nothing. Now, they massacre the entire town of Dresdin, and again, you all want to do nothing."

"The halflings owe us nothing, so their deaths are of little consequence to our financial holdings," replied another well-dressed councilman, who was obviously more concerned with trade and wealth than the lives of others.

It was another response from the council that made Villkir sick to his stomach.

"Are you worried about settling up on your debts? Are you not interested in helping someone unless their continued existence means the difference between your financial gain or loss? That is not what barbarians are about," Villkir said angrily.

"Correction," the fat council member said from his squatted, stressed chair, "that is not what barbarians used to be about. Or have you not been paying attention in recent years, Villkir? Trade and commerce have replaced war. Sure, there has been and will always be a need for a standing army to defend our investments, but barbarians today are merchants for the most part. And, as merchants, looking for ways to profit and protect ourselves from losses is what we do. Rushing off to fight a fight with unwinnable odds to defend the honor of the dead is not good for our profits. We do nothing because it costs us nothing and gives us the chance to profit later—the new barbarian way."

"Then, I propose this," Villkir said as he tried to desperately hold back the seething anger for the council that burned deep within him. "Let me ask for volunteers. Those willing to fight can, and those wishing to stay here and hope that their stacks of coins can protect them from the oncoming storm can hide behind the honor of their forefathers, since they will have none of their own."

But before the council could answer, Villkir added another final thought.

"And you have to let me send out messages to Mechii and Rhorm."

The council members huddled together and talked about Villkir's proposal for several seconds in hushed tones. He could see several times where various council members would angrily point in his direction or cast angry stares at him. He had obviously touched a nerve about their lack of honor, which was his goal, but whether it would work in his favor still remained to be seen.

Before the council could arrive at a decision, a young barbarian boy came running through the door, interrupting the proceedings.

"A message from Rishdel," the boy said as he handed the parchment to the fat councilman who had stepped around the table to intercept him.

The heavy-set council member unrolled the note and read it. A grimace settled across his face as he read its words before returning to the others still gathered around the table. The group spent the next couple of minutes quietly discussing the note and its contents, all while still pointing toward Villkir, who had no idea what the note could possibly say.

Villkir could hear the overweight councilman huffing loudly several times. He assumed the councilman disagreed with something being said each time. The thought of the councilman's opinion being discounted or overruled brought a small, discreet grin to Villkir's face. Villkir had long held that specific council member in contempt for his ongoing disrespect for the ways of the past.

Eventually, the group separated and Villkir could see the discontent in the pear-shaped council member's sneer at what the other council members were about to say.

"It would seem," the old councilman started, "that we are not alone in our awareness of this great and powerful force. The elves of Rishdel claim to have seen them as well as the group approached Kern. Obviously, this message is old, but it means that there are others who are concerned by the presence of just a large army whose leader and intent is unknown."

"Go and seek your volunteers, Villkir," the old barbarian continued. "We will respond to the elves to keep them updated on the force's recent activities and request their assistance. If we are to stand against them, we will need help, even if the help of elves is not what everyone wants."

He cast a judgmental eye in the direction of the overweight council member with that last statement.

"And we will send a bird to Rhorm..." quickly added another of the council members before being rudely interrupted by the fat one.

"But not to Mechii," he huffed. "If what your scouts say is true, then our bird will not reach them in time and it is already too late for those pesky gnomes. It would be a waste of a good bird."

"Very well," Villkir simply replied.

He was relieved to have the support from the majority of the council members. He even relished the idea of going against the wishes of the lumpy one. And while he was disappointed that they would not send a bird to Mechii, he could not argue that it was unlikely to arrive in time to serve as an advance warning. As much as it pained Villkir to admit, it would be a waste to send a bird to Mechii now. All Villkir could do was hope to gather enough people willing to fight and make it to Mechii to help the gnomes in their defense from the invaders. That was if they could make it to Mechii before the gnomes suffered a fate similar to their halfling neighbors.

***

"Grand Master Aldiri[8]!" the gnome shouted as he raced toward down the hallway. "The barrier spells are holding the perimeter, but the mages at the gate are not sure they can hold the encroaching beasts much longer."

The gnome city of Mechii was long ago placed inside a protective barrier spell that kept out uninvited guests, falling projectiles, and even inclement weather. It had allowed the gnomes to conduct their experiments and, in fact, their lives in relative peace without fear of disruption or contamination from the outside world.

The spell was originally cast in case of fighting between the races shortly after the great division of Corsallis so many years ago, but no war came. Now, however, the barrier was being put to the test. The

---

[8] Pronounced "Al-dear-e"

catapults and ballistae of the invaders rained down a constant barrage of rocks, bolts, and other miscellaneous objects onto the city. The barrier held strong as it deflected the projectiles, some of which were on fire, and protected the city's buildings and inhabitants from harm.

The only area of the city not protected by the barrier spell was, or at least thought to be, the city's single point of entry. This space had intentionally been left unprotected so that the spell would not constantly have to be dispelled and recast as people moved in and out of the city. From time to time, a similar spell would be cast to cover the opening, but that spell lacked the power and full protective capabilities of the old magic. At the first sign of the invading force, mages guarding the entrance cast their shielding spells, but it did not hold long against the non-stop assault from those outside.

Once that spell had been broken, the throngs of humans and dark elves that made up the invasion force for Mechii fought to make their way inside. They were, however, met with great resistance as a bevy of mages quickly swarmed the area and began furiously casting a multitude of spells. There were fireballs, firewalls, tornados, earthquakes, water spouts, and all kinds of other elemental spells being hurled at the city's attackers.

It was a defense of futility it seemed, though, as more and more trespassers only seemed to take the place of those defeated by the mages and their spells. Even with the growing number of gnomes now collected around the opening, the act of drawing the runes and casting the spells was taking too much time and allowing more and more of their assailants time to get closer and closer to their position.

Eventually, the gnome defenders were forced to retreat as they continued trying to cast spells. With each step further away from the gate they took, more of their new enemies encroached into the city. And as more and more space opened up between the gnomes and the entrance, the more the pillagers could spread out and mount more effective attacks on the gnomes. It did not take long for those first gnomes to begin falling under the blades, hammers, and arrows of the marauders. But, just like with the attackers, there seemed to be an endless supply of gnomes to take the places of those who had fallen.

And so, the fight for Mechii raged on.

***

Dhun and Bror watched from the distance as the large force split into two and the larger force turned toward Mechii, while the smaller, maybe one-third of the whole group, continued south, possibly toward

Rhorm—the two barbarians correctly assumed. From their vantage

point, they could see the ripples and shockwaves in the barrier spells as

the invaders tried in vain to penetrate the protective spell with their

numerous projectiles. Dhun and Bror just watched in awe as the

gnomes' magic repelled the gargantuan objects with ease and quickly

realized that the gnomes were a greater force than previously thought.

Perhaps there was a chance that the small creatures might survive.

But as the pair watched from the distance, they began to notice

the surge at the front of the group that had amassed near the city's gate.

The assault had breached the gnomes' defenses, and the unknown

troops began to pour into the city. Slowly at first, but over time more

and more began to flood inside more quickly. It was only a matter of

time before the gnomes would be overwhelmed by the invaders'

superior numbers, and they knew it.

It was time for the two barbarians to make a decision. Would

they wait and watch for the inevitable end, as Dhun had done at

Dresdin, or would they act like the barbarians of old and charge into

the fight, unafraid of death in the name of honor and right?

Their answer—a mix of the two.

First, they agreed to pass on a quick message to the nearest runner to inform the council back in Barbos of the attack on Mechii and to let them know that Dhun and Bror were attempting to aid the gnomes in their fight. Then, they agreed to put honor before their own wellbeing and finally take up arms against the marauders.

They wanted Barbos to know of their actions just in case they did not survive. They hoped Barbos would send reinforcements so that their impending sacrifices would be for something rather than nothing. Bror and Dhun knew that two barbarians against such a horde was not a fight that they could win, but perhaps they could start the fight that their fellow barbarians could end.

Bror, being the faster of the two barbarians, sprinted off to tell the runners of their plan. Meanwhile, Dhun stayed to watch the fight as it continued to unfold and come up with a plan on how the two lone barbarians could best help the besieged gnomes.

There was no easy option for Dhun. There were hundreds of the marauders below where he sat observing. Their best option was to mount a surprise attack from behind and try to catch as many of the horde by surprise as they could. But it was when he was studying the group's rear line that he found the perfect choice of targets.

Bror returned shortly, out of breath, and listened to Dhun's plan as he worked to recover the stamina that he knew all too well he would soon need.

"Look there," Dhun said, while pointing to the various siege weapons positioned at the back of the attack. "Those positions have virtually no defenders except the people using them. I say we hit those first."

Bror studying the different catapults and ballistae that Dhun had pointed out.

"Yeah, I see what you mean," he agreed. "I think that each of us can take a ballista with ease."

"And then..." started Dhun before Bror interrupted him.

"We use those ballistae to take down the catapults and maybe some of the ones charging the city," Bror said, mirroring Dhun's thoughts.

"Exactly!" Dhun said with a giant grin on his face.

The duo were of similar minds. They would take out the people manning the ballistae before using the invaders' own weapons against them. It was not without challenge, and once discovered, it would not take long for the two barbarians to be overwhelmed, but neither cared. They figured that if they could split the fight into two fronts, their positions to the rear and the city's gate, then perhaps they could buy the gnomes inside Mechii some time to beat back the forces that had made it inside the barrier and maybe even set up new defenses to turn back the attackers entirely. Bror and Dhun's main goal was to buy the gnomes of Mechii enough time for the barbarians to make it from Barbos to assist and hopefully spare them from the same fate as the halflings at Dresdin.

With their plan set, the two pulled their razor-sharp axes from their belts and rushed down the cliff's edge toward their targets below.

Little did the pair know of the recent developments in Barbos and that help was already on the way.

Chapter 12

Riorik, Kirin, and Nordahs had rushed through the forest and off

toward Tyleco. They wanted to meet up with Ammudien and Rory but

were unsure of how or where. The trio discussed trying to get inside the

city's towering walls and ask around for them but thought better of

such an idea, since they did not know if the gnome and human's visit

had gone as well as theirs. Little did they know of the current pursuit of

their friends by Tyleco's military at the behest of the city's supreme

leader.

The trio eventually came to the site of their battle with the bandits, gnolls, and Whilem at the bandit camp just west of Tyleco. The buzzards and other wild animals had already been feasting on the corpses that still littered the area. The stench of rotting flesh and excrement was pungent. Regardless, Riorik and Nordahs led Kirin to the entrance in the floor of the crumbling tower that led down into the tomb where they had previously found the greaves that were still firmly in Riorik's possession.

The two friends regaled Kirin with the stories from the fight, Riorik's near poisoned end, Asbin's hidden fury that was unleashed on Whilem's face, and how it all led to Wuffred's discovery of the shield sitting in Tyleco's armory. Kirin just shook his head in disbelief at all that he heard. It just seemed too much to be true, and if true, he was struck by just how close Riorik had come to death. Riorik and Nordahs were persistent about their story's truth so that eventually the wizard stopped accusing them of grand elaborations and accepted their very factual retelling of those very recent events.

Kirin was overcome by his emotions as he embraced Riorik and apologized profusely for not having been there to help him, saying that he now felt somewhat responsible for what happened to his brother.

Riorik tried to reassure his brother that he was fine and that he did not

hold Kirin responsible for their father's misguided ambitions.

"I probably would have done the same thing if he had reached

out to me," Riorik said to his softly sobbing brother as he tried to

console Kirin.

Riorik's words did little to wash away the guilt Kirin was feeling

at that moment, but he did appreciate his little brother's attempt.

After Kirin's emotions settled, the three continued to pass the

time telling stories. Some by Riorik and Nordahs about their Ranger

training or time with Wuffred. Some by Kirin about his experiences

with the gnomes in Mechii. Others were just tales about when one or

two of them did something funny, daring, or dangerous that the third

knew nothing of until now. It was just a relaxed conversation between

friends that, for the moment, allowed all three to forget about the

dangers they were all about to face.

After a few hours of waiting for their friends and telling stories,

the threesome decided it was time to move on.

"If they were on the run from anyone or looking for a place to

hide, this would have been the most logical choice. I think it is safe to assume that they're okay and still lingering somewhere inside the city," Nordahs eventually suggested to his friends.

"Do we think it would be okay for us to try and go through the gates to look for them now?" Kirin questioned, still hesitant to be around others, given his recent affiliation with their current opposition.

"Wuffred did say that he told the guards that they had been helped by some elves. Perhaps if we told them we were those elves and wanted to check on Wuffred, then the guards would give us welcome entrance into the city instead of the usual rude rebuff that others have reported over the years," Nordahs added.

"I don't know," said Riorik, still concerned about approaching the guards without knowing how Ammudien and Rory's meeting had gone. "I still think it is risky to associate ourselves with anyone else until we know the opinions others have of them."

"Then what else would you suggest, brother?" Kirin snapped at Riorik, aggravated by his brother's hesitation.

"What if," Riorik began to answer, "we head toward Kern as ordered? We can stay close to Kern in case we need to seek shelter there, but at the same time, maybe find Ammudien and Rory in case they were forced to go elsewhere outside the city."

"I wouldn't blame them if they did. The smell here is terrible," said Kirin as he retched, thanks to the pervasive miasma that had begun to waft into the tomb's entrance carried on a fresh breeze blowing across the area.

"Yeah, on second thought, I'm good with the idea of going to look for them somewhere far from here," concurred Nordahs, while trying to shield his nose from the horrid smell with his glove, an effort that was in vain for the poor elf.

"If nothing else, we can at least see what condition Kern is in and how they might have fared against Father's army," Riorik added, also trying desperately to prevent the clinging stench from entering his nostrils but finding no success.

With their eyes watering and their noses pinched shut, the three elves attempted to escape the smell of death that had settled over the area like an impenetrable fog. Riorik, Nordahs, and Kirin headed south, the nearest direction leading away from the bodies and the sickening smell that accompanied them. Their plan was to circle around the southern side of Tyleco as they made their way to Kern. They could only hope to find Ammudien and Rory along the way.

**

"Oh my! Oh my! It's horrible! What they did to them was terrible!" Toby shouted as he suddenly and violently awoke from his exhausted slumber.

The restrained human struggled against the leather straps that still held him in place. His head darted back and forth as he fearfully tried to take in his surroundings and evaluate his current predicament.

"Hush now," suggested the old barbarian medic as he rushed to Toby's side with a drinking bowl full of fresh, cold water from the nearby stream.

"You collapsed and need to drink. Here," the medic told him as he cradled Toby's head and poured the refreshing liquid into the human's mouth.

Toby gratefully gulped the water down. It did not take long for him to drain the bowl's contents, barely spilling a single drop.

"We have to get out of here," Toby eventually said once he had swallowed the last sip of water and caught his breath once more.

"Slow down," encouraged the medic. "You're not making any sense. Start from the beginning and tell me what happened."

Toby took a few deep breaths to calm himself before describing how the city of Kern was surrounded, the brutality of the gnolls just outside the gate, Lord Shiron's escape plan, and how he witnessed the slaughter of the others from a distance before making his way to Barbos.

"I fully expected the beasts to find and kill me. I ran all the way here but had to stop and rest several times. I didn't know what else to do or where else to go," Toby added.

"Well, you are here now. A few days have passed, and there are things you should know," the medic replied.

The old barbarian healer slowly and calmly told Toby about how the scouts had seen the troops Toby described moving south. He talked about the reported annihilation of Dresdin and how in light of those recent events, Villkir was assembling a force of barbarian fighters to go after the heartless invaders.

"You have to stop them," Toby begged the aged doctor. "They will be but lambs to the slaughter. Our only choice is to surrender and hope that they show us mercy."

Toby quickly became agitated and upset again at the thought of the barbarians making a futile effort to fight the marauders. It was suicide to the increasingly manic human.

"It is too late for that, I'm afraid," the healer replied, while he tried to calm Toby again. "After what was witnessed at Dresdin, I don't think mercy will be given to anyone. If Lord Shiron thought mercy was possible, would he have opted to flee the city? Did you see mercy offered to your friends as they fled Kern? Surrender only brings about our deaths quicker and without honor. That is not the barbarian way. No, our people will fight to the last breath to defend our honor, our city, our people, and our freedom."

The two continued to talk about the current events of the land. Toby maintained his attitude of helplessness, while his caretaker tried to offer counterpoints to Toby's emotions. The old barbarian wanted Toby to remain calm, so he offered words of hope and courage, but Toby's trauma ran deeper than he could reach, it seemed.

All the while, the sounds of barbarians talking and moving could be heard just outside the healer's home as Villkir was gathering his own force to confront the horde.

***

Bror and Dhun charged at their target ballistae. Each of the barbarians had circled around to approach from the rear. The humans and dark elves manning the large wooden weapons were so focused on continuing to pound the barrier protecting Mechii that none of them noticed the big, burly barbarians as they drew nearer. The element of surprise was with Bror and Dhun, just as they had hoped.

Bror reached the first two-man team operating the siege weapon. One worked to wind the winch used to draw the firing mechanism back under enough force to fling the heavy, bronze-tipped bolt over the ground troops and into the city, or at least until it struck the magical shield over the city. The other huffed and puffed as he singlehandedly lifted the heavy projectile with its long, sturdy wooden shaft combined with the heavy bronze tip, shaped for piercing whatever targets got in its way.

Bror wasted no time dispatching the operator with the projectile weighing him down. The powerful barbarian quickly ran toward the encumbered dark elf, who could not hear the barbarian's approach over his own labored breathing. Bror used the elf's noises for cover and was

239

able to get directly behind his target before wedging his axe's blade firmly into the rear of the elf's head.

It was an instant kill for the barbarian. Bror's powerful arms easily forced the axe's sharp blade through the elf's long, black hair and skull before coming to rest deep inside the brain. The dark elf's body immediately grew stiff from the shock of the blow before his muscles fell limp and he dropped the projectile back to the ground. Bror's opponent did not get the chance to make a sound or even look upon his killer's face. The quick attack left Bror undetected and free to make another surprise attack against the only other individual there, the dark elf still straining against the winch to get the last few clicks needed to fully wind the weapon.

This time, Bror slowly moved into position behind the lone dark elf and watched as the elf struggled to finish his job.

"You could at least lend me a hand," the dark elf complained aloud, thinking his companion was still alive.

"Let me help you with that," Bror replied, to the dark elf's surprise.

But before the dark elf could turn around to look at the strange voice's source, Bror firmly gripped the dark elf's shoulder, holding him in place with a single hand, and with his other hand, slammed his axe squarely into the center of the elf's back. The sharp blade sliced cleanly through the elf's spine as it buried itself deep into the flesh. The paralyzed elf could only grunt and groan as the pain spread throughout his body that was now going into shock. Bror continued to hold the elf up and in position as he slowly wrenched the blood-soaked axe head from the elf's body.

Once his blade was free, Bror released his grip on the elf, letting the elf's partially divided body fall helplessly to the ground. The seriously wounded elf was not yet dead though. Bror knew that if he did nothing, his foe would eventually die, but the barbarian dared not let his enemy live any longer than possible out of fear that the elf could still somehow disrupt his plans. So, with another single blow, Bror cleaved the downed elf's head free from his shoulders, extinguishing what life the dark-skinned elf had left.

With the ballista's crew dead, Bror, almost effortlessly, worked the winch to secure the final pull of the rope as taut as possible for maximum firepower. Then, where the other elf had struggled to carry

241

the weapon's bolt, Bror lifted the projectile with a single arm before casually placing it into the slotted rail used to hold and aim the bullet before firing.

His first objective now complete, Bror took a moment to carry a few crates of bolts from the nearby supply wagon over next to the weapon. He knew that once he started firing on the enemy troops, that time would be critical if he were to get off more than one shot, so he needed all the equipment as close as possible to where he was.

Bror now controlled one of the two ballistae. It was locked and loaded, and all that was left to do was use the weapon. The barbarian flexed his muscles and swung the weapon around so that it pointed at the nearest catapult. He took a quick moment to aim the weapon as best as he could, considering that he had never used one in combat before. Then, he pulled the clip that released the rope that propelled forward at a high-rate speed, pushing the bolt from the slotted timber rail and through the air toward his target. The bolt flew with such force that it sailed over his target and into the darkness.

Luckily for Bror, the catapult's crew were also so focused on their tasks that none of them noticed the errant shot. This meant that he could get the next bolt loaded and ready without any worries, which he promptly set about doing.

Meanwhile, Dhun was finding similar success at his target. However, unlike Bror, Dhun arrived after the ballista's crew had completed winding up and loading their weapon. The two crewmen were busy trying to aim their weapon as the barbarian crept closer. The two crewmen had been systematically firing at different places, looking for weaknesses in the city's shield. So now, as Dhun contemplated his attack, the pair were working to adjust their target.

Dhun figured that his best chance was before they fired the weapon, because once the bolt was on its way, the pair of elves would be free to combat him. His best chance for success was to attack, and hopefully kill, one of the crew before they were alerted to his presence.

Dhun crouched down and stealthily approached the dark elf reaching for the clip that would release the weapon's firing mechanism. Before the elf could fire the ballista, Dhun hacked at the back of one of the elf's knees. The elf immediately crumbled to the ground, but not quietly. The dark elf cried out in pain, as would be expected. This caused the other dark elf to turn and look toward his companion. But instead of looking at the pained face of another dark elf, the dark elf saw only the charging frame of a massive barbarian quickly approaching.

Dhun wrapped his muscular arms around the dark elf and squeezed him tightly before tackling the surprised elf to the ground. The barbarian aggressor quickly placed one hand over the elf's mouth and partially stood up as he raised his other hand with the axe in full display to his downed opponent. The other dark elf rolled around on the ground, clutching his severely wounded leg, while Dhun's latest target flailed about desperately, trying to grab ahold of the barbarian's arm holding to the axe. Dhun quickly solved that problem by pinning the dark elf's nearest arm to the ground under one of his feet. The dark elf's single arm was no match for Dhun's arm, but the elf continued struggling.

Dhun quickly grew tired of the dark elf's fight, and the barbarian severed the problematic limb at the elf's elbow with a single swipe of the axe. The dark elf tried to scream in pain, but Dhun's hand completely covered the elf's mouth. Only a very muffled noise was emitted. Dhun knew that he could not continue this fight long and that he needed to return to the other elf before he managed to fire the ballista. With the elf trapped and unable to mount a defense, Dhun made quick work of the dark elf by driving the axe's edge between two ribs, being sure to slice through the lung. This was followed up with another powerful swing, and this time the axe crunched through the chest bone protecting the center of the elf's body. As the barbarian's blade pushed through the bone and into the organs normally protected behind it, blood spurted from the wound, covering Dhun's arms, hands, and axe.

Satisfied that he had completed that task, Dhun returned to the first elf, who was now attempting to pull himself up from the ground using the many levels of wood making up the ballista. The elf had managed to get himself about halfway back up before Dhun's attention turned back in his direction.

Dhun, eager to stop the dark elf's ascent, tossed his axe the few feet between him and the dark elf. The weapon expertly tumbled through the air before sticking into the weapon's wooden frame, right where one of the dark elf's hands had been. The strike cleanly separated the elf's fingers from his hand. This caused the elf to lose his grip and fall back to the ground, shouting in even more pain than before.

The barbarian pounced on the downed elf. He began pummeling the elf with his fists out of frustration, afraid that the elf's cries would draw some very unwanted attention to Dhun's position. It did not take too many hits from the strong barbarian to render the elf unconscious.

All that was left to do was for Dhun to dispose of the elf.

Dhun decided to make an example of his barely breathing foe.

The ballista was loaded and ready to fire, but first, Dhun hung the unconscious dark elf from the end of the weapon, just in front of the giant projectile. The barbarian torqued the weapon so it faced a nearby trebuchet that had recently hurled a huge boulder at the city. He fired the weapon, releasing the bronze-tipped bolt that easily drove through the hanging dark elf before both the elf and the bolt took flight toward the other weapon.

Dhun's aim was on point. The over-sized arrow drove itself through a human standing near the trebuchet's side before firmly burying itself in between the teeth of the gear that was used to crank the weapon's basket into position. The shot rendered his target useless now that the gear was securely blocked. But more than that, the sight of two impaled companions sent a shock among the others crewing the towering siege machine, especially as they tried to comprehend where the second body came from.

Dhun's success did not cause him to stop, though. The barbarian quickly worked to reload his new weapon and aim it at the trebuchet's crew, who were still scurrying about trying to understand what had happened. He fired another shot, but this one just missed its mark as it buried its tip deep into the ground. Dhun's position and intentions were now revealed, and the very angry crew began to rush toward his ballista. He tried to get off as many shots as he could but was only able to take out one of the several humans who had manned the weapon now headed his way.

As the charging humans drew too close for the ballista to hit, Dhun grabbed his axe once more and readied himself for another round of close-quarters fighting.

***

Rory and Ammudien arrived just outside of Kern. They could easily tell where Cyrel's forces had been located just by looking at the trash left behind, the sheer number of footprints that covered the area, and the trail of blood leading toward the city's northern gate. The pair followed the blood trail just long enough to find the impaled corpse of Lord Shiron, still sitting on full display for the people of Kern just outside the city wall.

"It is as I feared," Ammudien began. "This is a clear sign that Kern did not repel Cyrel's army."

"Do you think anyone else survived?" Rory worryingly asked his friend.

"Without entering the city, I cannot say," the mage answered. "I detected the presence of movement in the city consistent with the movements of people, but I cannot discern one individual from another, so I have no way of knowing if the movement was that of a resident or an invader."

"Then what should we do?" the usually confident and take-charge guard captain asked, lost in the viciousness put on display in front of him.

"We move south," Ammudien replied. "That way, since Lord Veyron will undoubtedly be tracking us, he will find Lord Shiron here and either stop to help Kern or continue his pursuit of us that will lead him to Cyrel's horde. Whether he wants to help or not, we will not give him much choice if he wants to find us," Ammudien added with a smirk.

"And what about Riorik and Nordahs? How will they find us now?" Rory, obviously ignorant of Ranger skills, asked.

"They are trained trackers. They never needed my magic to see what was near. My magic only was able to see what was too far for even their eyes to see. I have no doubts that they will find us in time. The real question should not be how they will find us but when will they find us."

The gnome's answer did little to calm some of the fears brewing in Rory's mind, but the human was relieved to hear that his new elven friends had the skills that would help them come to Rory's location.

Being mindful of Lord Veyron's pursuit, the odd couple wasted no time lingering in the open. They began making their way south to trail the dark army and hoped with each step that they would soon find themselves reunited with the remaining members of their party.

Chapter 13

Lord Veyron and his horsemen arrived at Kern shortly behind Rory

and Ammudien's departure. The much faster horses were allowing the

eager ruler and his troops to quickly catch up to their prey. But, just like

with Rory and Ammudien, the unexpected sight of Lord Shiron

skewered by the spear, now caked and covered with dried blood, caused

the whole group to stop and pause.

"It serves him right," Lord Veyron initially huffed at his distant

family member's death.

His disregard for Lord Shiron's death was quickly replaced by an irrepressible sadness at his cousin's torturous death at the hands of such brutal people.

"Well, perhaps he deserved better," Lord Veyron eventually said, countering his previous sentiment.

"Take him down," the finely dressed Veyron ordered his men.

The other riders quickly dismounted and moved to where the spear's handle had been driven into the ground by the troll. It took several seconds for the men to study the scene in a sense of awe at how the spear had come to rest there. They knew little of the raw power possessed by trolls that could apply such tremendous force.

After several of the men had offered suggestions on how to go about freeing Lord Shiron's body from the spear, they eventually come to the conclusion that they would have to use their blades to chop the spear's wooden shaft in two and lower the top part that contained Lord Veyron's slain relative to the ground. The blood that encapsulated the spear's shaft made it very slippery, preventing them from simply pulling the spear from the ground intact.

But before the soldiers from Tyleco could do anything, a voice rang out from the distance.

"You there! Stop!" shouted the voice.

Every one of the men, Lord Veyron included, looked in the direction of the voice. A small detachment of armed men walked toward them, exiting Kern's gate.

"Do not touch that!" another of the men shouted at Lord Veyron's men.

It was apparent that the people did not want Lord Shiron's body being disturbed, despite its dishonorable condition.

"What is the meaning of this?" Lord Veyron demanded of the dissenters.

"Lord Shiron was a coward who fled the city and left us to die. His ending was befitting a person of his moral emptiness, and our continued existence is predicated on his continued display of shame," answered the man seemingly leading the group still marching undeterred toward Lord Veyron and his more heavily and better-armed soldiers.

"Who is responsible for this man's death?" Lord Veyron questioned as the group stopped just shy of Lord Veyron's location.

"The Dark Lord of Narsdin," answered the group's leader.

"And who is that?" Lord Veyron asked, his voice full of disdain and sarcasm for having to ask such an obvious question, at least obvious to him.

"He who leads the northern region's army. A force larger and more capable than any other single army in existence," replied the scrawny man just beside the leader before being elbowed in the gut by the said leader.

"Hush now," the leader quietly instructed the other man.

"Who wants to know, is the better question." the leader huffed with contempt, unfamiliar with Lord Veyron or his family's crest that emblazoned his shield and the banners that his men bore on their saddles.

"I am only the rightful heir to the throne and the leader of Tyleco, Lord Veyron. Lord Shiron was my cousin. Do you still think his death befitting a man of his heritage?"

"Not if he had acted with honor, but honor seems to have been lost on him," the man told Lord Veyron with a sense of defiance.

"I see," started Lord Veyron. "And to speak against the dead, especially the man responsible for all that you have gained since birth, is without honor. As such, do you think it would also be befitting for you if I had my men execute you and your little band of followers in a similar fashion, then leave your bodies to rot in the daylight as a warning against such insolence?"

It was at this point that the group actually took stock of just how many of Lord Veyron's men stood around them and just how much better the soldiers from Tyleco were equipped compared to their ragged clothes and rusted makeshift weapons fashioned from old farm tools. A lump quickly formed in the angry leader's throat. It was his pride and ego that he was now forced to swallow before it got him and his friends killed in a fight that would be no contest for the well-trained soldiers.

"My apologies, Lord Veyron," the man quickly said, trying to reverse the damage his previous words had done. "It was wrong of me to speak so ill of the dead. But, alas, we still cannot allow you to take down this symbol of our oppressor's control. To do so would incur the wrath of his troops upon their return. Our people have pledged loyalty to the horde's leader in exchange for our lives. Any opposition to his will have severe consequences that none here wish to know. If you want to honor your cousin, then you will have to do what we could not

and repel the invader's forces, which are significant."

The man's words echoed in Lord Veyron's ears as the leader

recalled Ammudien's warning and description of the army the gnome

had claimed to have seen. It was now clear to Lord Veyron that

Ammudien had told him the truth. This did little to assuage the desire

to retrieve the shield in Ammudien's possession and the anger at the

gnome's brazen theft of the shield. But it meant that Lord Veyron now

had a choice to make. He would either continue his pursuit of

Ammudien and Rory or march his forces into war against the so-called

'Dark Lord of Narsdin'.

As luck would have it though, the answer to this question was

soon revealed that he could do both. Under additional questioning by

Lord Veyron's soldiers, the group all concurred that the evil army had

headed south, the same direction that it was believed Ammudien and

Rory had fled. This was a win-win for Lord Veyron, who arrogantly

assumed that he could recover the shield from the thieving gnome

along the way to leading his army, the biggest known army among the

noble races, into battle against this mysterious foe's forces before

returning to Tyleco victorious—just as his predecessors had, and which was surely to give him the support needed to finally the claim the throne as his own and obtain the title of king that he felt he so rightfully deserved.

Lord Veyron ordered his men to return to their mounts before issuing a stern warning to the men from Kern to do what they must to preserve Lord Shiron's corpse for a proper burial when everything was over. He wanted to threaten the men but felt that given how they had described their oppressor that to do so would make him no better than the unknown foe he was now off to fight. Instead, he offered them incentives in the form of money, something the men would gladly accept in exchange for their efforts.

Then, just as quickly as they had arrived, Lord Veyron led his troop of horsemen away from Kern and toward the raging battle still unfolding at Mechii.

***

Riorik, Nordahs, and Kirin had been moving quickly as they skirted around the southern side of Tyleco. Their fast pace had them already deep into the sand dune fields that extended south from the Narsdin region and between Tyleco and Kern. Their sharp elven eyes could already begin to make out the shapes of Kern's wall rising from the horizon off in the distance. They would reach the human settlement soon.

But they had yet to see a single sign of Ammudien and Rory. The Rangers had noticed some odd shards of glass and a stone that certainly looked out of place to the town's eastern edge, but the trio chose to ignore the unusual scene so that they could keep their pace. Little did they know that what they had stumbled across was Ammudien and Rory's crash site from their exciting and magical escape from Lord Veyron.

The shifting sands of the dunes tried to slow their speed, but the quick steps and light-footedness of the elves allowed them to continue with the same sense of urgency on the sand as they had moved when on the more solid ground. Each step they made barely disturbed the soft sand. If anyone had tried tracking the elves through the sands, then they would have had an almost impossible time following them. It was completely opposite of the difficult, trudging pace that Baolba, U'gik, and their band of gnolls and orcs had been forced to endure when they crossed through here several weeks earlier.

In what seemed like no time, the trio had crossed a good portion of the sandy sea and held Kern firmly in their sights. But more than that, the elves with their vastly superior vision could now make out shapes of people moving along the road leading away from Kern. It appeared that two groups were making their way from the city.

The first group was only two people, one tall and one short. Their thoughts instantly were of Ammudien and Rory. The human and gnome would have that appearance from a distance. Unfortunately, though their eyes were good, the elves were still too far away to discern any details that may help them identify who they were seeing. It was possible that they only spied a parent walking with their child, they had no way of knowing for sure without getting closer.

The second group though, due to the nature of the group, was easier to identify. The children of the forest could easily make out the shapes of horses with riders on them. Was this part of Cyrel's army chasing after the first group? Was it part of a defense force from Kern riding out to fight or protect the pair ahead of them? Despite knowing that it was a group of mounted riders, there was little else they could make out from there.

Their only choice was to continue moving in the direction of Kern. The closer the trio approached the city, the more details they would be able to discover about the groups. And with each step the groups grew more and more in focus until finally they were revealed.

It was Kirin that first made out the robes Ammudien wore. As a fellow magic user and former student of the Mage Academy, Kirin was very familiar with how a gnome in the robes looks, even at a distance. But it was Riorik and Nordahs that recognized the banner of Lord Veyron adorning the many horses that rode behind them. The two elves had spent enough time near Tyleco throughout their quest to recognize that crest, and it did not take much imagination to draw the correct conclusion that it was not a friendly pursuit that they were witnessing.

The elves casually but quickly changed direction. Their new course was an intercept course that would ideally put them between the riders and their friends. The only question was whether or not the elves could cover that much ground before the horses caught up to the others. At first glance, the horses were going to win that race.

The elves' pace quickened, transforming into an all-out sprint. Still, it did not seem enough. Nordahs quickly evaluated the situation in

259

his head and figured that they would be too late, but only by mere seconds unless something happened to slow the pursuers.

"I have an idea," Nordahs said to his friends between his controlled breathing.

"Kirin," he said to the wizard, "I need you to stop and cast a spell to slow those horses down, otherwise we won't make it there in time. Do you think you can cast something that far?"

"I don't know that I can cast something that far, but I might be able to create enough noise to draw their attention, at least for a few seconds. Will that work?"

"Perfect," Nordahs answered. "We just need to buy Ammudien and Rory some time. And Riorik too."

"Me? What do I need time for?" a confused Riorik questioned.

"To put on the greaves. Then you can use your enhanced speed to get from here to there more quickly as you did at the oasis."

"I don't see how three against that will have any different outcome than two against that unless you have some other tricks planned," Riorik replied, unconvinced by his friend's plan.

"I will still be right behind, just slower. Plus, your brother will continue casting spells. We both know now how effective magic can be against a group. Remember what Ammudien did at the tomb when we first met him? Kirin knows just as much as Ammudien, if not more, so his magic will make up for our smaller number. We just have to get there fast enough to give Ammudien and Rory a chance. Once Ammudien and Kirin both start casting spells, I bet you and I can just sit back and watch."

"I think you give me too much credit," Kirin interjected as he continued scribbling some runes in the air.

Regardless, Nordahs had convinced Riorik that it was worth a try. The elf quickly dropped his pack, fished the greaves out from its depths, and set about pulling the legendary armor over his legs once more. The armor clung to his hips, thighs, and calves as if they had been tailored specifically to him. The magical ability to automatically adopt a form-hugging fit still amazed Riorik.

Equipped and feeling the surge of energy coursing through his legs, Riorik bolted away from their position with almost lightning fast speed. Nordahs could barely see his friend as he tried, but failed, to keep up with him.

In the distance, the horses and their riders were almost right on top of their prey. Many of the soldiers had readied their swords to strike their targets as they galloped past. But before they could go in for the kill, a loud, thunderous crack rang out as the sky lit up brighter than the brightest part of the day. The light blinded all who saw it, not just the horses and riders in Lord Veyron's party.

Luckily, Riorik and Nordahs had their backs to the light, so they were spared the temporary disability. It was not what they had expected from Kirin, but it was certainly effective and bought them the time needed. Riorik arrived between the two groups several seconds ahead of Nordahs, who eventually joined him. They stood and looked on as the horses tossed and turned their heads, some throwing their riders from their mounts. Lord Veyron's men had come to a complete halt thanks to Kirin's unexpected blast.

"Rory! Ammudien!" Riorik called out to their friends, who had also been stunned by the spell's effect.

"Rio? Is that you?" Ammudien called back.

The gnome was grateful to hear his friend's voice. And it helped him to quickly understand what had happened. The mage immediately knew which spell Kirin had cast to cause such disarray, although he was not sure how Kirin made it so powerful. But, now that Ammudien knew the spell, he knew how to counter its effects.

The gnome set about drawing a quick set of runes near his face before waving his wand from side to side in front of his nose. His spell seemed to wipe away the blinding light that filled his eyes before. Now, Ammudien could not only hear his friends but also see them.

The mage hurried to Rory and performed the same spell to free his human ally from the debilitating spell.

"They didn't look friendly, so we decided to intervene," Nordahs said as he cast a welcoming smile to Ammudien.

"Oh, they are not friendly," Ammudien answered. "I tried to tell Lord Veyron about Cyrel's army, but he only wanted to covet the shield while the world burned around him, so I was forced to take the shield and flee. Only, he refused to give up on stealing my people's shield another time."

It was about this time that Kirin's spell began to dissipate, and some of the soldiers started getting their vision back and their horses under control. Nordahs was the first to ready his weapon by notching an arrow and pulling his bow to a full draw. Riorik, having stopped by the armory at the Rangers Guild before leaving, readied his two shiny short swords. Ammudien withdrew his wand from his sleeve and stood ready to begin casting spells as quickly as he could manage. Rory, who had been disarmed at Tyleco, stood with his bare fists clenched, ready to go down swinging.

"Don't be silly, Rory," Nordahs said. "You won't manage well like that. Come take one of my daggers. Give yourself a chance at least."

Rory did not appreciate Nordahs' assessment of his odds but did not argue with the elf. He stepped over to Nordahs and took one of the curved kukri [9] shaped daggers from his belt.

Lord Veyron, whose vision had fully returned now, looked at the pair of elves now standing next to Rory and Ammudien. The racist human hated the elves almost as much as he hated Ammudien for stealing what he felt was his shield. The elves had never done anything to Lord Veyron, but he was raised to consider the elves as arrogant elitists who looked down upon anyone who was not an elf. It was a bit ironic, considering how he viewed the people under his rule as well as

---

[9] Pronounced "Coo-kree"

the other races compared to himself. The irony was lost on him though and, at that moment, all he wanted to do was kill the four of them, not knowing that Kirin was still approaching from his flank.

"Kill these detestable elves and their friends!" Lord Veyron shouted. "I will not be denied what is mine!"

"It is not yours, and it never was!" Ammudien shouted back. "This shield belonged to my people before you humans stole it!"

"Charge!" Lord Veyron screamed as he kicked his horse's side with his feet to spur the beast forward.

The foursome of friends readied to defend themselves, but before the men and their horses could cover the short distance to them, a wall of flames erupted from the ground and stretched well beyond the sides of the charging cavalry. The intense heat of the flames burned some of the horses and men closest to the point of eruption, including Lord Veyron. The pain of singed flesh caused the group to retreat away from the wall.

"What do you think of that?" Kirin asked with a giant grin on his face as he ran up to his friends.

"We don't have long, it only divides us, it does not box them in or anything," he added.

"What do we do? Do we run?" Rory asked, still a little unsure of what magic had to offer.

"Oh wait, watch this," Kirin giggled as he drew some new runes and pushed them toward the flaming wall.

The runes approached the wall but never touched it. Instead, the runes seemed to be pushing the wall as the burning blockade glided over the ground and toward the group of soldiers on horseback.

The mounted riders furiously tried to escape the encroaching inferno. Many of them turned and retreated on the road toward Kern. Some, either by their choice or by the choice of their mount, instead tried to flee across the sand dunes. This did not end well for most as the panicked horses struggled with the weight of their riders in the soft sand. A few of them were even burned by the wall as it passed over their position and continued to chase the bulk of the group away.

"Now we run," Kirin told the others.

There was no discussion. Everyone secured their weapons, turned away from the wall, and took off running.

"Why didn't you just kill them?" asked Rory, a little disappointed that the spell had not done more to the very men he used to call friends but now hunted him.

"Because we are going to need Lord Veyron's forces if we are to win this war," Kirin answered flatly, unaware of the events in Tyleco.

Rory did not respond to Kirin, but everyone heard his defiant grunt as they ran.

"But more importantly," interrupted Ammudien before Rory's disgruntled attitude could be expressed more, "how did you make that wall move?"

"Just a simple wind spell to push the fire," answered Kirin. "The firewall spell contains the flames into that shape, so the wind just pushes the flame's container."

"That is most interesting," Ammudien said, still in awe of the effectiveness of Kirin's basic spells.

"Magic is full of combinations like that, which take two basic spells from different schools and use them together for a more powerful effect," Kirin added.

"And is that how you created such a bright flash like that? A combination of magic?" Ammudien asked, curious to learn more about the wizard's secrets.

"No, nothing that heretical," Kirin said with a laugh. "I just stacked the runes for the same spell several times on top of one another so that when I cast it, they all went off together and caused a bigger effect."

"Wow!" exclaimed the surprised gnome. "I did not realize that you could do that. I always thought it was one spell at a time."

"Well, technically it is," replied Kirin. "If I had tried to cast a different spell before I had cast those runes, then they would have faded to give way to the new spell, but because it was the same spell just repeated, I was able to stack them like I did."

"Where were you two going?" Riorik asked his friends, who he had seen headed this way earlier.

The elf knew that if he did not ask the question now that he might not have a chance later as Kirin and Ammudien were still chatting about various spells and mystic arts. The two casters met under tense conditions, but recent events bonded them, and apparently, it sparked what would be lengthy conversations in which the others could not participate due to their supreme lack of knowledge and training.

"Just south," replied Rory. "Ammudien felt your father's troops heading South with his magic, so our plan was to lead Lord Veyron to them."

"So, why was he chasing you like that?" asked a curious Nordahs.

"He didn't want to help Kern because of his ongoing feud with the other lords about who is the rightful heir but was intent on taking back Sagrim's Shield from Ammudien. And, apparently, Lord Veyron was led to believe that I was somehow involved in the initial plot to steal it, so I have been branded a traitor and am now being hunted for a crime I did not commit."

"Well, welcome to the club of miscreants and vagabonds," teased Riorik. "But seriously, where are we headed now?"

Ammudien broke from his chat with Kirin to answer Riorik's question.

"Lord Veyron does not strike me as someone so easily turned away from something such as this. Kirin's moving wall of fire will certainly slow them down, but he will, without a doubt, resume his chase—and with renewed vigor now. We should continue South until we find Cyrel's army because when Lord Veyron stumbles across their path, the two will have no choice but to fight because both will want what is in between them—our pieces of the armor."

***

"Is this it? Are no more barbarians willing to fight?" Villkir asked himself as he stood in front of the gathering of volunteers.

Villkir had gone door to door to every home and shop in Barbos to drum up support for his volunteer squad. But, in a town of only a few hundred barbarians, he managed to only find roughly fifty willing to join his cause. Many of the others were too old or too young to join, but the number was much lower than Villkir had expected from those capable of fighting. He wondered if perhaps the barbarian spirit of their forefathers had truly been replaced by the new love of money.

Disappointed but undeterred, Villkir knew that time was of the essence, especially as word of Bror and Dhun's plans had just reached him. He knew he could wait no longer to see if maybe anyone else arrived. Villkir cleared his throat as he prepared to address the small group of barbarians.

"Every one of you has come here today to volunteer to stand up to tyranny and avenge the genocidal slaying of the peaceful halflings. I know that you all have no doubt heard the reports of the size of the force that we are about to go against. It is true, we will be outnumbered. But we will not be outfought. No force on this land can compare to the might of a single barbarian, much less a band of barbarians who fight for a common cause. No matter the odds, we will be victorious!"

There was a cheer from the group. Villkir's speech was not the most uplifting speech, but those who volunteered needed little in the way of encouragement or inspiration to fight.

"Barbarian strong! Barbarian proud!" Villkir yelled back to their cheers.

The group repeated his words and it quickly became a chant, a war cry of sorts, as the small army of barbarians marched through the streets and toward the mountain trail to war.

Chapter 14

The horde's smaller group was closing in on the dwarven city of

Rhorm. The horde's leader had anticipated fighting the stout dwarves in

the caves and mines where they had made their homes in the ore-rich

mountains that dominated the southeastern corner of Corsallis. So, with

that in mind, the group headed toward Rhorm consisted mainly of

gnolls, wargs, and dark elves; all vicious fighters who could see in the

dark tunnels while remaining nimble enough to fight effectively in

cramped spaces.

Unfortunately for them, not only had the dwarves received the warning from Rishdel before the army's arrival, but the dwarves had felt the marching mass's feet as they sent tremors through the rocks and ground that the dwarves were so intimately attuned to. This meant that the dwarven army was prepared and had planned a surprise for the marching invaders.

Before the collection of furry gnolls, hairy wargs, and dark elves with their glowing eyes could reach the mountain town of Rhorm, they were set upon by the dwarves, who had been lying in wait.

The ambush was completely unexpected. It quickly caused chaos to spread as the wargs, who were more domesticated pets than sentient being like the gnolls, scrambled in all directions. Their handlers tried in vain to control the overgrown beasts, but the wargs' survival instincts were stronger than their handlers' voices and commands. The directionless wargs ran amok through the remaining group, which caused the gnolls and dark elves to scatter or be trampled by the larger wargs.

Adding to the chaos, the dwarves were using weapons unlike anything the troops from the north had ever encountered before. There were loud bangs, flashes of light, tons of smoke, and all that somehow caused a barrage of small objects to fly over the battlefield. The dwarves had developed a form of basic gunpowder using the materials mined from the area and with it had created simple firearms that could shoot several lead balls over a great distance with deadly force. It was the Dwarven Blunderbuss, a weapon that would later go on to dominate battles as more and more armies adopted it, further increasing the dwarves' riches.

The dwarves put their new experimental weapons to good use. Instead of aiming at the rampaging wargs, the dwarven marksmen continued to frighten the wargs by discharging their weapons and taking out those around them. Scores of dark elves and gnolls fell to the devastating impacts from the lead shot deployed from the booming muzzles of the dwarven guns. The continued bombardment from the flashes, smoke, and explosion from the gunpowder kept the invaders in a state of constant disarray and confusion.

It did not take long for most of the marauders to be riddled with holes and litter the ground with their corpses. The only chances that they had to fight back were when the blunderbusses caused the entire area to be filled with smoke. The dwarves were then forced to stop firing to allow the smoke to clear so that they could see their targets once more. Though still dizzy from the array of unexpected stimuli, the Dark Lord's forces did their best to counter the dwarves and their guerrilla tactics.

With each pause between attacks from the dwarves, those who had not been shot did their best to rush their ambushers. Several were gunned down as they moved into a point-blank range of the armed dwarves, who were no longer blinded by the smoke over the battlefield. But some did manage to reach the hiding spots where the dwarves had been firing from. In one case, a dark elf even managed to take a blunderbuss from the dwarf that wielded it. Unfortunately for that dark elf, he did not know how to operate the strange contraption, and the dwarf grabbed his battle hammer that was strapped to his back before using it to club the confounded dark elf to death.

After only a few minutes of fighting, it was apparent to the invaders that the attack on Rhorm had failed. And not by a little bit, but completely and miserably.

The group's leader, the armored elf now known as The Dark Lord of the North, had stayed at Mechii to oversee the assault on the gnomes. He had expected Rhorm to fall as easily as Kern, so no true leader had been appointed for this task. As such, the dark elves who had survived yelled for a retreat while the gnolls howled and growled in anger to attack. In the end, no orders were followed fully either way, and the group fractured even more. It made the dwarves' jobs that much easier. Those fleeing were left to run away while the dwarven gunners focused on taking aim at the ones who had remained.

The assault on Rhorm never really began, and only moments after it had started, the dwarven ambush was over. The dwarves had dominated the fight in an overwhelming display of force, thanks to their new gunpowder-fueled handcannons. But the dwarves were not content with their lopsided victory at home and vowed to chase those that had fled back to their main force for a final showdown.

The dwarves were fiercely territorial and despised the idea that anyone would force them from their home, snatch away their mines, and worst of all, rob of them of their much beloved golden money. Gold was the ultimate prize for the dwarves. It represented wealth and ore, the two things they held dear. Many dwarves had an unhealthy obsession with the shiny metal and would fight in an instant, even against other dwarves, if they thought someone was trying to take it away from them. The very real threat of oppression, occupation, and death spurred the dwarves to fight with all the fight Rhorm could muster so that they could avoid losing that which was closest to their hearts.

***

"Look there, just up ahead," Riorik told his friends as he pointed to the shapes in the distance.

"What do you think that is?" asked Kirin.

"I don't know," replied Nordahs and Riorik simultaneously.

The three elves were straining their eyes to see as far ahead as possible, but their tired eyes just could not make out enough details still to see the small band of barbarians descending the mountain trail.

"Do you think that's all that remains of your father's army?" questioned Nordahs.

"Surely not," answered Riorik. "The army we saw by the oasis was huge, and we have not passed by enough dead bodies to think that it has been reduced to only a few dozen already."

"I guess we will find out for sure soon," said Kirin.

Rory and Ammudien, not as quick and agile as their elven friends, had fallen behind a bit and with their average vision could not see what Riorik, Nordahs, and Kirin did. All the poor gnome and human could do was continue to chase their friends and hope that they were not left behind. In fact, the gap between them was large enough that Rory and Ammudien could not hear their discussion about who might be on the trail ahead of them. Rory and Ammudien carried on, blissfully unaware that they were approaching what could be another hostile force.

***

"Villkir, do you see what I see?" asked Endol[10], the barbarian nearest Villkir at the bottom of the mountain trail.

Villkir had not been looking in the same direction as Endol, so his question caught Villkir by surprise.

"What do you mean? What do you see?" Villkir asked back.

"It looks like someone approaches from the north. I thought the scouts said the troops had already moved past Barbos toward the South," Endol replied.

Villkir immediately whipped his head around and looked to the north. He had been so focused on what Bror and Dhun had reported to

---

[10] Pronounced "In-doll"

the south and their plans to help the gnomes that he did not bother to consider that anyone could still be to the north. Then his mind flashed back to the message from Tyleco about how they had heard stories of the large army moving in this direction and the council's response informing Tyleco of the army's advancement past Barbos. He wondered if the people coming into view were reinforcements from the well-defended human city.

"Let's go figure out who they are and see if they mean to harm us, rather than turn our back to them and expose ourselves out of something as foolish as faith," Villkir directed those now under his command.

The small tribe of barbarians who had planned on going toward Mechii now turned in the opposite direction and headed north. With the two groups on a direct course toward one another, it did not take long for them to get a good look at one each other. It was apparent at first glance that with three elves, a gnome, and only one human that this was not reinforcements from Tyleco, and so the question in Villkir's mind remained, who were these people?

"Stop and identify yourselves," Villkir demanded as he held his giant two-handed sword out and turned sideways as if to represent a gate or a roadblock.

Riorik and the others came to a stop several feet away from the bigger group of larger, stronger individuals. The elves recognized the barbarians after their encounter with Whilem and immediately understood the threat that one of them represented individually. As a group, they were far more than the Rangers felt comfortable fighting, even with the help of two magic users. By keeping distance between the two groups, the two Rangers felt it would give them enough time to react and defend themselves and their friends if this meeting turned out to be an unfriendly one.

"I am Riorik Leafwalker of Rishdel and a Ranger of the Order," Riorik said with a confident and stern tone.

He wanted to convey a sense of authority and importance to the barbarians, hoping that it might give them a reason to pause before attacking him if they thought he was someone special.

"And that means what here?" Villkir shot back, obviously unimpressed by Riorik's introduction.

Such a response caused Riorik's nerves to get a bit frazzled. It was not a warm welcome by any stretch of the imagination, but at least nobody had tried to stab or cut anyone with a sword yet. The friendliness of the barbarians was still an open question for the elf and his friends.

Riorik wanted to offer a rebuttal to Villkir's dismissive question but was drawing a blank on what to say. Fortunately, the elf did not have to worry about that long because Ammudien spoke out against the barbarian once his short legs carried him to where everyone else had stopped.

"I suppose it means nothing to a bunch of merchants such as yourselves," quipped Ammudien between breaths.

"But, if you must know," the gnome continued, "these brave four are accompanying me to Mechii. We have good reason to believe that my hometown is under attack, and they have vowed to help me defend it. As such, for your lot, I suppose you would consider Mechii 'closed for business' for the time being, and you will have to seek your fortunes elsewhere."

The gnome's angry tone was not what Riorik had hoped for, but he dared not to interrupt the angry mage after seeing the damage Ammudien was capable of.

"I think what my friend means," Riorik said, thinking it better to clarify the mage's words before one of the barbarians stomped on the gnome in anger, "is that a large army was headed toward Mechii, and we go to aid the gnomes in defending their homes."

Villkir, annoyed that Ammudien's tone that had been somewhat like his own earlier, quickly decided that the five people standing in front of him were of little threat to his pack of combat-ready barbarian volunteers. And since there was no real threat, the lead barbarian decided a little tact would not hurt, especially given that they were also headed to Mechii to confront the same foe.

"I must say, that is most surprising," Villkir began. "We are not merchants as the little one suggests. No, we are fighters, just like you, headed to confront the very force you also oppose. Our only fear is that we will not be quick enough, since our scouts have already reported that the assault on Mechii has begun."

The news sent chills down the spines of the small group of friends but more importantly, changed Ammudien's attitude from one of dislike for the barbarian to one of fear and concern for his fellow gnomes.

"What?" Ammudien fearfully asked. "It has? When? Are the barrier spells holding?"

The flurry of questions and sound of absolute terror and concern in his voice broke down Villkir's emotional walls as well. The large barbarian lowered his sword and knelt before the wide-eyed gnome.

"I cannot say what is happening now, but the last I heard, the barriers were holding, and your people were holding their own against the massive forces stacked at their gates. There is still hope, little one, but we must hurry if we are to be of any assistance and stop what happened to Dresdin from happening again at Mechii."

Villkir's words brought some relief to Ammudien, but the gnome did not know what the barbarian meant about stopping what happened at Dresdin from happening to Mechii. It seemed as if more had happened than they had known while off trying to find support in the other towns. But the updated news sparked a thought for Nordahs.

"Excuse me, good barbarian, sir," Nordahs said, trying to address Villkir despite not knowing his name yet. "Could you get word to Rishdel of these events? Our elders remain unconvinced that any real threat looms, so this information is imperative to secure the Ranger Guild's support."

"Oh, and you must ask them for help," Riorik quickly added. "The elders will not send help unless it is asked for."

The proud barbarian initially balked at Nordahs' request. It was only after he overheard the murmurings from the barbarians behind him talking about needing all the help they could get against such numbers did Villkir relent.

"Yes, I will send someone to fly a bird to Rishdel with news," Villkir eventually agreed. "But if you wish to accompany us to Mechii, then I must insist that we leave now."

Riorik and the others quickly agreed to join the barbarian squad since they shared a common goal. There was still some hesitation about being around barbarians after Whilem's attempt to take the greaves for himself, but the group figured that if they all were headed to Mechii, then any such betrayals would happen there just as well. At least if they all traveled to Mechii together, then there was a chance for some bonding that might prevent such greedy, lustful acts with maybe a few of the barbarian. And who knows, maybe those barbarians would help defend Riorik or Ammudien from less honorable barbarians that tried to take what was not theirs.

Villkir, being a person of his word, sent a runner back to Barbos to get a message to Rishdel informing the elders of the recent news and ask for their assistance in defeating this 'newest plague to swarm across their lands'. But the lead barbarian was quick to muster everyone together and get the pack moving south toward Mechii once more.

Only the barbarian did not notice that another had decided to follow his group. Behind the group trailed a large mountain goat with thick, fluffy white hair and long, pointy horns sticking up almost straight into the air from atop its head. The billy goat was careful to always stay several yards behind the group's movements but was following the group.

***

By now, Lord Veyron's troops had caught up to the retreating horsemen. The army, now together in its entirety, paused to address the many minor burn wounds and even a few severe ones that had been suffered by the men and their horses thanks to Kirin's floating wall of fire. The incendiary blockade had served its purpose quite well and not only had allowed for the group of friends to escape but had also put some extra distance between them and their pursuers. This was the last thing that Lord Veyron wanted, but he was determined to continue hunting Ammudien and the shield.

"Hurry up!" Lord Veyron barked once his wounds, which were minor, had been cleaned and dressed by the medics.

"Do not waste time on the inevitable or the insignificant," he bellowed.

Lord Veyron was certain to have all his wounds addressed but felt it a waste of time to give his men the same level of care. Capturing Ammudien and retrieving the shield were a greater priority to the covetous lord than the health of his own men. He needed his men healthy to see the chase through, but Lord Veyron's thoughts were so clouded with anger and desire that he failed to see this.

Nevertheless, his men followed his orders and before long, the hunt was on once more. This time, the horsemen did not gallop away though. This time, the group stayed together and moved as a single unit, except for some of the riders taking turns acting as forward scouts who rode ahead of the rest looking for signs of Ammudien and Rory's trail.

It did not take long for the group to return to where their previous encounter had occurred. The ground was scorched from the flaming wall's intense heat. There were even some patches of dry grass that still smoldered and smoked from the wall's presence. The few charred remains of horses and men who could not escape the wall's hotness still emitted heat as the troops passed by. It was the sickening smell of burnt hair and meat that filled the nostrils of every man there. The group could not pass this area by quick enough, although they tried.

Once past the blackened bodies of their colleagues, the group was thankful for the fresh air that blew across the open fields. And more importantly, one of the advanced scouts returned with news. It was not the good news that Lord Veyron had hoped for though.

"Their tracks are very fresh," began the scout.

This news brought an eager smile to Lord Veyron's face. He knew that his prize was close and was confident that it would be his again by morning.

"But," the scout continued, "it appears that they may have met up with others outside of Barbos, possibly some barbarians judging by the size of the tracks."

This information did not please Lord Veyron in the slightest. With only three new friends, Ammudien, Rory, and the shield had not only managed to elude capture but had managed to inflict serious wounds on Lord Veyron's cavalry. The thought of his prey having even more help now was most concerning, especially if that help was from barbarians, who were known to be bigger, stronger, and meaner than anybody in Lord Veyron's army.

"How many barbarians?" Lord Veyron asked, thinking that there might be only one or two barbarians that his men would have to contend with when they caught up to them.

"There were a lot of tracks, Lord Veyron," the scout answered.

"So, what, four? Five?" Lord Veyron pressed the scout.

"No, my lord," the answer replied. "I could easily detect the tracks of more than a dozen different barbarians, but looking at the surrounding area and the impact the group had as they moved, I would suspect that the number would be closer to twenty or thirty at least."

The number was closer to fifty, but between that many feet moving about over the same area in such a short period of time, it was just too muddled for the scout to accurately assess. Either way, the scout was able to correctly determine that the so-called 'fugitives' they were following were now in the company of several barbarians, making their task even more daunting than before. It was not news Lord Veyron welcomed, but it was still unclear if the barbarians had taken the others prisoner or if they were all working together.

Lord Veyron was still undeterred. He chose to believe that the barbarians had captured Ammudien, Rory, and the others instead of befriending them. He did not want to think about the notion of the barbarians being involved in his fantasy plot against him.

Over the course of the pursuit, Lord Veyron had concocted an elaborate fantasy to explain everything. He had convinced himself that Rory plotted with Ammudien to steal the shield so that Rory could usurp power from Lord Veyron before trying to claim the throne for himself. The elves, he now believed, were helping Rory in an effort to have the former guard captain installed as a puppet ruler under their influence. And now, with the addition of the barbarians into the fray, he felt the barbarians must be on his side since humans and barbarians were more closely related than barbarians and elves. If he could find the barbarians, then he just knew that he could finally recover the shield and see the conspirators punished for their crimes.

Lord Veyron's delusions were beginning to take a toll on his grasp of reality.

Chapter 15

The troops outside of Mechii continued their attempts to breach the city's defenses. For most of the ground troops, they did not notice the gradual decline of aerial bombardments from their siege weapons. There was hardly a single projectile still striking the barrier covering the city. Bror and Dhun had successfully attacked most of the massive structures placed at the rear of the assault.

But their attack was not without consequences. Both barbarians had suffered injuries. With each new target, they would invite the wrath of the crew operating the siege engines. Each time the powerful barbarian fighters were able to overcome each wave of attackers, but the constant fighting had begun to take its toll on them. Their breathing was becoming labored as their stamina faded. Their arms and legs moved more slowly as their muscles burned in agony at the growing lack of energy. This meant that their opponents were able to find more and more success in defending against Bror and Dhun's attacks while landing more of their own.

Bror had taken a spear tip to his left shoulder, rendering that arm virtually useless and a great source of pain for the barbarian. With every movement, the disabled limb ached and burned thanks to the open hole now in his arm. At first, the wound gushed blood profusely, but the red liquid turned white after a few seconds, and the blood was quickly replaced by a foamy puss-like substance. The change in the wound's excretions both terrified and angered the barbarian. He fought on, more as a response to the adrenaline that surged through this body more than anything else.

Dhun had likewise taken abuse from the defending troops. A sword had pierced his belly, leaving a deep gash in his abdomen. Dhun had seen such wounds kill others, but not quickly. Such wounds were known as "the walking death" as it could take days for someone with such an injury to finally succumb to the wound, and there was little any medic could do to spare them from such an end. The barbarian knew his time was limited now, but he vowed to make the most of what life he had left. Dhun was determined to die victorious or die trying. There was no honor in giving up just because he was hurt. Dhun could still fight, so it was his duty to do so.

Despite their injuries, the two barbarians had managed to take out all but one catapult. The other siege weapons had been placed to the flanks of this final weapon in the center. Neither of the barbarians was aware of how the other had fared to this point. Each hoped for the best but feared the worst for their friend. But, as luck would have it, the two approached the final catapult at roughly the same time.

Dhun was the first to arrive from his side and without being noticed by the bustling crew. He carried a large bolt from one of the ballistae in one hand and a sword that he had taken from one of the fallen defenders after getting his axe stuck in another's face. Even with his wounded gut and fading energy, Dhun thrust his weapons at his foes with power and authority. He managed to impale two of the catapult's crew with the ballista's bolt. Unfortunately, he could not free

293

the bodies from the weapon since the tip had hooked edges designed to penetrate and stick into walls and armor. He was forced to abandon the bolt and carry on with just the sword.

Bror arrived next, just seconds after Dhun's initial attack. The large catapult's crew, now alerted to Dhun's presence, had started to rush to Dhun's side to fight off the barbarian, unaware of the danger that approached with Bror's arrival. With his one good arm, Bror carried a large chunk of wood from one of the siege engines he had smashed previously. His axe's blade had chipped badly after colliding with other weapons wielded by his opponents, and what parts of his blade that had not chipped had dulled after the repeated strikes against his various targets.

Thanks to his large frame, long arm, and the sheer length of the wood he carried, Bror was able to swing the giant piece of timber in a sweeping arc across his body. The wooden weapon slammed into one of the humans running to defend against Dhun's assault on the other side. The blow knocked the human into the catapult's frame before he was squashed between the frame and the barbarian's makeshift weapon.

The sound of the collision between human and frame then weapon to human was disturbing. At first, there was an audible thud as the human's head bounced off the solid timbers that held the catapult in place followed by a loud, exasperating cough from the human as the impact forcefully expelled every ounce of air from his lungs. Next, there was the dull slap on the wood as it hit the human's soft, squishy flesh. Then finally, the cracking and snapping of bone from the force of the two kinds of wood essentially squeezing the human in between them like a vice.

This caught the attention of the remaining crew, who were now forced to divide their efforts between the two barbarians. Three of the crew were already dead, so this left only three more to take on their larger assailants. Two turned toward Dhun, leaving the last to confront the more noticeably wounded Bror. The three crew members wasted no time calling out for help, but with the other crews already dead and the frontline trying to push forward away from the catapult's position, there was nobody near enough to hear their desperate pleas.

The remaining crew was alone, and if they wanted to survive, they would have to take on the powerful presence of not one but two barbarians.

The lone defender tasked with taking on the wounded Bror charged directly at his opponent. Bror struggled to pull back his wooden weapon in time to make another sweeping attack. The charging human saw the barbarian's attack with ample time to roll under the flying timber and continue his charge.

Bror was not as lucky. In his haste to make the attack, the barbarian swung the wooden log with all his might but had not set his feet. The force of the swing and the lack of a collision caused the timber to arc wider than Bror had anticipated. His one good arm was unable to counter the torque of the attack's momentum, leaving the makeshift weapon to spin Bror around so that his back was now to his attacker. It was a guaranteed death sentence, and the barbarian knew it and knew that there was nothing he could do about it in his current condition.

The human rushed at the defenseless barbarian and thrust the tip of his sword through Bror's back. The blade's sharp point and edges easily penetrated through the barbarian's clothes, flesh, and muscle. Bror could only cry out in pain as the sword slid through his body before protruding through his chest. The human had driven the sword fully into Bror's back, stopping only when the top of the sword's hilt, the guard, was flush with the barbarian's lightweight, cloth clothing.

The shock from the pain immobilized Bror at first, but he quickly recovered his senses. Knowing that he was done, Bror reached behind him with his good arm after dropping the splintered timber and grabbed the human's wrist. The human struggled to free himself from Bror's grip, but the barbarian squeezed with all his remaining strength.

Bror then pulled the human's hands free from the sword's handle. Still, the human struggled in vain to release himself from the barbarian's grasp, but it was not to be. With a single yank, Bror spun the human around from behind him to in front of him, forcing the human's back to also become transfixed on the sword's blade. The human's eyes opened wide, almost bulging from their sockets from the shock and pain of being stabbed by his own weapon. Bror wrapped his good arm around the human's shoulders and with his last gasp of air pulled the human backward down the blade so that the two fighters were hip to hip. With his lifeforce drained, Bror collapsed forward to the ground, trapping the skewered human between the ground and his own fresh corpse.

Meanwhile, on the opposite side of the catapult, Dhun, with his painful stomach wound, was finding more success defending himself from his two attackers. With the sword being his only remaining weapon, the barbarian managed to deflect several of the strikes from his opponents and their weapons. In one case, one of the human crew members rushed at Dhun. Dhun used his weapon to knock the human's attack away and followed his successful defensive maneuver with a strong left hook that landed squarely on the human's jaw before knocking the stunned human to the ground.

That punch bought Dhun the time he needed to even the odds. The force of the punch had not only sent its target tumbling to the ground but had distracted the other crew member, who stopped and stared at his stunned ally in a state of surprise at the barbarian's power. Dhun made the most of the advantage he had created by running to the onlooking crewman and using his free arm, pinning the human against the catapult's frame with his forearm before driving his sword's tip into the man's left side and through his heart. He pulled the blade from the wound and quickly delivered a second, similar strike, just for good measure.

Now, all that remained was the lone crewman, who was still shaking his head in an attempt to regain his senses after being hit by the strong barbarian. Again, Dhun was fast to recognize his enemy's dazed condition and the opportunity it created for him. He held his sword so that the pommel was at the top,, and the blade's edge ran along his arm as he ran toward his target. And, with what energy Dhun's muscles could still muster, he lifted his arm fast and hard, sending the sword's edge slicing deep from the catapult's last defender's groin all the way through his chest,, nearly slicing the human in half.

The human just stood there, nearly motionless, for a few seconds. His arms and fingers twitched, his eyes blinked quickly, his body seemed to almost tremble. Eventually, the human fell to his knees without a whimper before collapsing face first into the ground.

Dhun had survived their suicidal attack on the siege engines, much to his surprise. He sighed in relief, despite the knowledge that his wounds were most likely lethal. But, before he could think about his own mortality further, his thoughts flashed to Bror.

Dhun dashed to the opposite side of the catapult. He saw his friend lying dead on the ground after having been stabbed in the back. At first, he was saddened by the sight of his dead friend and fellow barbarian, but this sadness was quickly replaced by rage. All that Dhun could think about was how to inflict more carnage against those that have now taken the life of his friend.

The obvious answer was the massive catapult standing nearby.

Dhun struggled to operate the bizarre weapon by himself and with his injuries, but he was eventually able to both wind the gears that powered the catapult's arm and then load the weapon's basket with the largest boulder he could manage from the nearby supply cart.

Once the weapon was primed and ready, Dhun guessed at how to aim the contraption. His goal was to hurl the heavy boulder into the middle of the troops still anxiously trying to get into Mechii's well-defended gate. After a quick moment of assumptions and analysis of the odd weapon, the barbarian pulled the lever he assumed would launch the weapon's projectile.

His assumption was correct.

The catapult's basket vaulted forward, flinging the large rock in its basket in a high, shallow arc through the air. As the boulder reached its flight's crest, it came crashing to the ground with great speed and whistled as it pushed the air around it aside with tremendous force.

The flying stone slammed into the ground just yards away from the self-appointed king as it crushed several of his troops and sent debris flying in every direction, causing collateral damage to others. It was the first time that the Dark Lord of the North had noticed the lack of attacks from the siege weapons. This close call immediately drew his attention to the rear of his army to watch for activity. It did not take long for him to notice, in part to his improved vision, that many of the siege engines had been demolished or disabled. There was obviously an opposing force at work there.

The northern king quickly dispatched a small detachment of soldiers to protect his army's rear. And more importantly, to prevent anyone else from nearly burying him under a boulder from his own weapons.

***

The group ordered to regain control of what was left of the siege weapons ran toward the position of the weapons. There were more than a hundred yards between them and the last standing catapult. It would take the armor-laden soldiers several seconds to cover that much ground before they could faceoff against their unknown opposition.

The assortment of humans, dark elves, gnolls, and orcs worked to quickly make their way toward where their master had indicated. But about the time the group reached halfway, their attention was drawn to a loud commotion to their left. The group stopped and looked at the few gnolls and dark elves running their way while screaming in obvious terror.

"Run away! Run away!" one of the dark elves shouted as he drew nearer his allies.

"Those nasty, fat dwarves' weapons burn," cried out a gnoll, referring to the hot lead balls shot from the booming blunderbusses.

"It was a trap," another dark elf yelled as he waved his arms in the air trying to warn the others. "They knew we were coming!"

"They're dead! Everyone else is dead!" exclaimed the first dark elf as he finally reached the other group.

"We are all that is left. The dwarves killed the rest with their demonic weapons," he added as he clutched and shook one of his dark elf brethren.

"What do you mean 'demonic weapons'?" the confused dark elf asked his terrified colleague.

"I don't know how to describe it," the dark elf started to answer. "It was like a handheld explosion with a flash of flame and tons of smoke, but out of the smoke shot dozens of small projectiles. If they hit you, you are dead."

"So, it's like a flaming arrow?" the dark elf asked, still unsure what to make of the other elf's description.

"No, you fool!" the first elf exclaimed. "Think of it more like a slingshot that can launch more than one stone at a time over a greater distance and with enough force to pass right through you. But, if that isn't good enough for you, just wait here and you can see for yourself. The dwarves and their nasty weapons are not far behind."

The dark elf turned loose of his fellow dark elf and pushed passed him and through the group of soldiers that had gathered around.

"And I'm not waiting around here to see it again," the dark elf shouted over his shoulder as he continued to flee north, away from the fight.

Many of the others who had returned from the ambush outside of Rhorm followed suit. The experience of the concussion-inducing booms from the thunderously loud weapons, the choking smoke that filled their lungs, and the nearly indescribable sight of seeing so many of the others in their group mowed down by the fire-breathing, lead-slinging weapons had left them shellshocked and completely uninterested in continuing the fight. Those survivors were headed home whether their lord and master approved or not.

This left the group ordered to secure the siege weapons with a conundrum. Do they worry about the dwarves and their new weapons or do they continue toward the catapult and other siege weapons to confront an unknown foe? Are the foes at the catapults the dwarves?

In the end, there was no time to think about it. They had been ordered by their vengeful leader to protect the siege weapons, so that was what the group was determined to do. There was little value in detouring to fight the dwarves if their master was only going to kill them later for disobeying his orders. And so, once more, the group headed off to cover the remaining distance between them and their objective.

***

Dhun worked through the sweat, pain, and blood to reload the catapult for a second shot. The lonely barbarian pulled against the wheel to crank the ropes that would lower and hold the bucket in place. For a barbarian free of injury and full of energy this might not have been much of a problem, but for Dhun it was a great challenge. Every part of his body ached from exhaustion, the gaping wound in his abdomen burned with each breath, and the now overwhelming sense of pain had the determined barbarian on the border of collapse. His vision faded in and out. He felt dizzy. But Dhun pushed on.

He focused on the task in front of him as he tried to push out any thoughts about his injuries, his tiredness, and even his inevitable demise. Dhun was trying to simply will himself to carry on, even though his body did not want to. The barbarian was so focused on trying to pull the heavy gear lever on the catapult's side that he did not notice the approaching footsteps of others.

The bloody and wounded barbarian pulled on the wheeled gear, but his hands slipped. Dhun was too tired to hold on to the gear's lever any longer. The gear began to spin forward, undoing what Dhun had worked so hard to accomplish. But, to his surprise, the gear suddenly stopped.

"Looks like you could use some help," a familiar voice said from the other side of the catapult.

A weary Dhun looked over to see Villkir turning the gear, restoring Dhun's lost work. The other barbarians rushed to Dhun's side and attempted to aid their wounded and bloodied friend. Relieved to see the other barbarians, Dhun finally relaxed and let his body slip into the unconsciousness that it had been fighting the stubborn barbarian over for the last several minutes. A couple of the barbarians carried their wounded, limp friend away from the catapult and began trying to dress his wounds while other barbarians filled the space he now left vacant.

With the power of multiple barbarians, Villkir's forces were able to quickly reload the catapult and get off another launch before being interrupted.

As the barbarians worked to prep the catapult for a third launch, the group looked up to see a small group of soldiers staring back at them. The barbarian force, with the addition of Riorik, Nordahs, Kirin, Ammudien, and Rory, was a larger force than what had been dispatched by their master. For the gnolls, dark elves, and humans, the sight of so many barbarians together was very daunting.

The only one among the group that seemed unconcerned by the oversized cousins of men was the lone orc.

The orc was of similar height compared to the barbarians but was built with a much sturdier frame. The orc was stronger than any one barbarian in a head-to-head fight, but the simpleminded orc was not taking into consideration the difference in numbers between it and the barbarians. The orc just knew that it was told to go fight, so that was what it was going to do.

After a brief but tense staredown between the two groups, the orc shoved the others aside as it made its way to the front. The barbarians opposite the orc readied their weapons while Riorik and the others stayed in the back, eager to watch the showdown unfold.

The orc raised its large iron club into the air and charged toward the barbarians.

The rampaging orc did not get far before a series of deafening booms were heard from the side of the conflict. Several small thuds could be heard striking the towering beast. With each hit, the orc seemed to be knocked more and more off balance before finally falling over under the barrage. Numerous small holes could be seen in the orc's thick hide with each hole oozing the thick, dark orc blood. The sudden, unexpected, and noisy death of the orc drew the attention of both sides, who turned simultaneously with stunned and confused expressions on their face to look at a line of dwarves surrounded by swirling smoke.

The dwarves who had just fired now stood behind the front line as they worked feverously to reload their muzzle-blasting blunderbusses. Behind them stood even more dwarves. Some were armed with more guns, but most carried more traditional weapons of war. It was clear that all Rhorm had come and were ready to fight.

Looking back and forth between the dwarves and the dead orc, the dark elf quickly realized why the others had fled without fear of their master's contempt. He too wanted to turn and flee in that exact moment but knew the time for running had passed. It was no longer a matter of fight or flight but one of fight or surrender. Neither was a promise of survival, and the dark elf was not entirely convinced by the looks in the eyes of the dwarves staring back at him over the barrels of their weapons that surrender was even an option.

He was soon proved right when the dwarves, without word or warning, unleashed another volley on the enemy's forces. Several of the dark elves, gnolls, and humans fell in a flash as the many lead balls

scattered over a wide area, hitting a wide group of foes. Some fell to the

ground dead, having been struck in the head or vital organs. Others

simply fell under the impact of the lead shot that left them with a

multitude of wounds of varying seriousness.

That line of dwarves now moved back behind the others, and

another line of dwarves took their spot. The new line of dwarves held

their blunderbusses and leveled the muzzles on the remaining foes.

Another blast from the guns filled the air with smoke and lead shot.

Any of those who had remained standing from the first two attacks

now laid on the ground dead or dying. It was apparent to the dwarves

and anyone watching that their new weapons were certainly devastating

against small groups of enemies when given enough time to fire and

reload the slow-firing weapons.

***

With the orc and its friends dead or incapacitated, the dwarves now

turned their attention to the barbarians. But, unlike the dark elves and

their allies, the dwarves did not just open fire on the barbarians, who

had obviously opposed the other group.

"Who goes there, and what business have you here?" a grumpy dwarf demanded of the barbarians now being held at gunpoint.

"I am Villkir," the lead barbarian said as he stepped forward. "We barbarians are here to do our part in forcing this evil from our homes. Our scouts watched as they slaughtered everyone in Dresdin without mercy, and we refuse to go so quietly into the afterlife."

"Same," replied the grumpy dwarf. "These foul beasts attempted to sneak into our homes, but we were ready. The elves of Rishdel had sent a warning that one of our own insisted we take to heart, having recently returned from spending time with a few of these elves."

The dwarf's mention of another dwarf recently returning caught Riorik's ear. Curiosity got the better of the elf who hurried forward past the barbarians and directly in the line of fire.

"Asbin? Are you talking about Asbin?" Riorik blurted out before he could think better of his actions.

"Yes. Asbin is the one," answered the dwarf. "And I assume based on your attire and her descriptions that you must be Riorik, correct?"

"That is correct, sir. I am indeed Riorik," the elf replied.

"And where is Wuffred?" the dwarf asked flatly.

Riorik looked down at the ground as he thought of his fallen friend. He wanted his friend to be recognized and honored for his efforts and sacrifice, but it seemed that everyone who they encountered held the berserker in contempt. And, based on the dwarf's tone, Riorik felt certain that this would be another of Wuffred's many detractors.

"He is dead, sir," Riorik answered solemnly. "We confronted this army's leader north of Kern. The army's leader was about to kill me, but Wuffred intervened. He died defending me, and I am alive today because of him."

"Hmph. So much for being a father to his half-breed child," the dwarf huffed.

"Excuse me, I don't think this is the time or place to discuss family issues," Villkir said, interrupting the exchange between Riorik and the dwarf. "We don't need to stand here and wait to be killed. We should be fighting them and not worried about each other."

"He's right," Riorik urged, casting a concerned look at the dwarf.

"Very well," the dwarf agreed. "You can explain Wuffred and Asbin to me later, elf!"

Looking back up at Villkir, the dwarf told him, "I need your people's size and strength on the front line with me. Let my people deal with this contraption while you and I go stain this field with the blood of our enemies."

The combined forces of the dwarves, the barbarians, Riorik, Nordahs, Kirin, Rory, and Ammudien turned and charged at the much larger force standing before them, still focused on the gnomes who continued to hold strong against the invader's advancements.

Printed in the USA
CPSIA information can be obtained
at www.ICGtesting.com
LVHW050330090224
771178LV00001B/53

9 798350 715651